CIMARRON DREW HIS .45—

He aimed the gun at the mound of buffalo robe. "Come out of there," he demanded.

When nothing moved, he jerked the robe away. Antelope, huddled on the ground, stared at him. "Warrior Woman has offered five ponies for me," she said sadly. "Take me with you instead."

Not knowing how to reply, Cimarron holstered his gun. At that, Antelope leaped to her feet and grabbed him.

"I don't want a woman. I want a man. I want *you!*" Frantically, she unbuckled his cartridge belt and then went to work on his shirt.

"You oughtn't be doing this—" he protested.

By now she had his shirt off and was working on the buttons of his jeans, and her busy hands soon silenced any further protest. . . .

SIGNET Westerns You'll Enjoy

(0451)

5 CIMARRON
AND THE ELK SOLDIERS

BY

LEO P. KELLEY

Ⓞ
A SIGNET BOOK
NEW AMERICAN LIBRARY
TIMES MIRROR

PUBLISHED BY
THE NEW AMERICAN LIBRARY
OF CANADA LIMITED

PUBLISHER'S NOTE

NAL BOOKS ARE AVAILABLE AT QUANTITY DISCOUNTS WHEN USED TO PROMOTE PRODUCTS OR SERVICES. FOR INFORMATION PLEASE WRITE TO PREMIUM MARKETING DIVISION, THE NEW AMERICAN LIBRARY, INC., 1633 BROADWAY, NEW YORK, NEW YORK 10019

The first chapter of this book appeared in *Cimarron in the Cherokee Strip*, the fourth volume in this series.

First Printing, September, 1983

2   3   4   5   6   7   8   9

 SIGNET TRADEMARK REG. U.S. PAT. OFF. AND FOREIGN COUNTRIES REGISTERED TRADEMARK - MARCA REGISTRADA HECHO EN WINNIPEG, CANADA

SIGNET, SIGNET CLASSIC, MENTOR, PLUME, MERIDIAN and NAL BOOKS are published in Canada by The New American Library of Canada, Limited, Scarborough, Ontario

PRINTED IN CANADA

COVER PRINTED IN U.S.A.

CIMARRON . . .

. . he was a man with a past he wanted to forget and a future uncertain at best and dangerous at worst. Men feared and secretly admired him. Women desired him. He roamed the Indian Territory with a Winchester '73 in his saddle scabbard, an Army Colt in his hip holster, and a bronc he had broken beneath him. He packed his guns loose, rode his horse hard, and no one dared throw gravel in his boots. Once he had an ordinary name like other men. But a tragic killing forced him to abandon it and he became known only as Cimarron. *Cimarron*, in Spanish, meant wild and unruly. It suited him. *Cimarron*.

1

The trail he was following suddenly veered to the left, so Cimarron turned the blood bay beneath him and rode south toward the ambling north fork of the Canadian River.

When he reached it, he rode out into the shallow water and, upon emerging on the opposite bank, searched along it in both directions until he found the spot where Jake Farley had ridden out of the river.

The hooves of Farley's horse had made three sharp impressions in the ground and one that was blunted, the latter the result of the shoe the animal had thrown, which Cimarron had found many miles back along the trail, one bent nail still clinging to it.

Farley was heading west now and Cimarron, judging by the spacing of Farley's mount's hoofprints, knew he was galloping. If he keeps up this pace, he thought, he's liable to find himself a man on foot before too long. He smiled.

He had not ridden far when he came to an expanse of dunes. The sand of which they were composed had once been part of the river bottom but now it lay unevenly humped under the bright July sun.

He kept as close to the riverbank as he could without losing sight of Farley's trail in order to avoid the dunes that would slow his pursuit by providing uncertain footing for his bay. But, as the westerly wind began to rise, it sent swirling up into the air particles of sand that stung his face and hands.

He pulled his blue bandanna up until it covered his nose and the lower part of his face and rode on, squinting down at Farley's trail, which was gradually being erased by the wind as it whipped across the surface of the dunes. But the trail was still visible when Cimarron left the dunes behind him and

7

continued riding west into a heavily timbered area that was dominated by black-barked oaks.

He pulled down his bandanna as the bay moved through the thick shadows of the densely packed trees, its hooves shattering some of the many brittle branches that littered the forest floor. Soon it emerged into an area of ragged sunlight that fell through the leafless branches of many dead trees.

Cimarron noted the holes and glyphs in the trees' trunks which had been made by boring beetles. The beetles had also begun to bore, he noticed, into other nearby oaks which, he knew, would ultimately succumb to the devastation wrought by the beetles as they bored between the bark and the wood of the still-living trees.

The bay moved out of the sun and into the cool shade of the forest again and, as it did so, Cimarron used his bandanna to wipe the sweat from his face. He bent down low over his horse's neck to avoid low-hanging branches and later, as the bay came out of the forest into the sun flooding the Osage Plains, he pulled his black slouch hat down low on his forehead and squinted into the distance.

The plain was covered with plants and grasses, all of them lusty with life beneath the sun that indiscriminately nourished them. Bunch grass predominated, but in places there were clusters of crested wheat grass, and Cimarron didn't miss the several broken stalks directly ahead of him. He began to move forward again, scanning the vast plain that stretched out around him and noting the crushed plants in his path, fleabane and dock among them.

He continued riding at a fast trot until he saw the low-growing branches of a wild rose bush ahead of him move and then become still. He halted the bay, his eyes on the bush.

Snake? He sat in his saddle, watching, and when a jackrabbit bounded up from beneath the rose bush where it had been lying, his eyes followed its erratic flight.

Something's wrong with that critter, he thought. Then he saw the dried blood on the animal's rear legs. Something almost got it, he thought. It's near to dead.

His stomach rumbled with hunger and he swallowed the saliva that suddenly filled his mouth. As the rabbit went to ground again, unable to continue its flight, he got out of the saddle and walked over to it.

When he reached the animal, it tried to rise, its eyes wide

with fright, but it could only stir slightly while its nose twitched and its front paws made feeble movements.

Cimarron stared down at it in disgust and disappointment. There were other wounds on the animal's body he now saw. Maggots squirmed in most of them. The critter's not fit to look at, let alone eat, he thought. He went back to the bay, swung into the saddle, and continued following Farley, occasionally dismounting to examine the ground for signs.

When he spotted horse droppings, he knew he was not far behind Farley because they were still moist despite the blazing heat of the merciless sun, which was wringing sweat from his face and body.

When the sun above him momentarily darkened, he looked up, expecting to see a cloud. There was none. But there was a golden eagle soaring in the sky and the bird, as it flew between Cimarron and the sun, had momentarily blocked the light. It flew high, its wings spread wide as it rode the updrafts, banking off them as elegantly and as effortlessly as if it were a part of the wind itself.

Cimarron reached behind him and his right hand closed on the stock of his booted '73 model center-fire Winchester.

But he let go of the rifle, his eyes following the flight of the eagle. You shoot, he warned himself silently, and the noise you make'll likely as not bring Jake Farley gunning for you if he's anywhere in the neighborhood.

But, he thought, I just might be able to turn that eagle into my dinner without firing a single shot. I've seen how the Indians do it. Maybe I can do it too.

He turned the bay and galloped back to where he had last seen the jackrabbit.

It was still there and still alive, but barely so. He slid out of the saddle, scooped it up, got back in the saddle, and rode for the hummocks that rose out of the plain a little to the south. When he reached them, he selected a shady spot between two of them that would give him cover and then he led the bay around behind the highest hummock and left it, its reins trailing, beneath a ragged outcropping. He rounded the hummock then and quickly tore up the grass and plants growing near it in order to expose the ground. He tossed them aside and then, after tying a piggin string he took from his saddle around the rabbit's front legs, he dropped the animal on the ground and, playing out the piggin string, he took

9

shelter in the shade between the hummocks. He lay belly down on the ground without moving except for his right hand, which did move as, hidden under his chest, it jerked the piggin string and the jackrabbit scampered along the ground as it tried to escape.

He turned his head slightly so that he could see the sky. He waited a moment and then jerked the piggin string again, watching as the eagle dipped sharply, then circled, its head angling sharply to one side.

He pulled the piggin string once more and then let go of it as the eagle came plummeting down toward the rabbit that was still struggling to free itself. As the great golden bird spread its wings wide to brake its descent and its talons opened to seize its prey, Cimarron's right arm shot out and seized one of the eagle's legs. The bird screeched and began to struggle, its curved yellow beak descending again and again to tear the flesh on the back of Cimarron's hand. He sprang to his feet and, as the eagle's wings flapped furiously and its feathers flew into the air, he deftly wrung its neck.

He dropped the bird then and watched its body flop about on the ground for several minutes, its wings shuddering and its talons convulsing, before it finally lay lifeless at his feet.

He picked up his kill by the legs and, after boarding the bay, rode for the river. When he reached it, he got out of the saddle and dropped the eagle into the cool water to rid it of its body heat, since he intended to skin and cook it immediately and he knew that body heat tended to give game a nauseating flavor.

He found a flat stone, pulled his knife from his right boot, and yanked the eagle out of the water. He girdled the skin of both legs with his knife, peeled the skin back, girdled the tail and anus, cut an abdominal incision from tail to rib cage, and then ripped the bird's internal organs free. He severed the bird's legs, wings, and head and then washed it in the river before gripping the bay's reins and walking to a stand of cedars where, using broken branches he found on the ground, he made a spit and then a fire with his flint and steel.

He hunkered down before the fire he had made, slowly turning the spitted eagle and blowing on the smoke rising from the fire to disperse it so that it would not betray his presence in the cedar grove. He looked up and was pleased to see that the tendrils of smoke that had escaped him were being dissipated among the leaves of the overhanging branches.

When the bird was a golden brown, he lifted the spit's crossbar with both hands and began to eat, tearing hungrily at the roasted flesh with his teeth and hardly taking time to chew as he sought to appease the hunger that was so strong within him.

When he had finished eating, no shred of meat remained on the bony carcass that he tossed into the flames, causing them to spit and crackle as they consumed the grease on the bones they quickly began to char.

He rose and kicked out his fire, drank from his canteen, and then climbed aboard the bay and rode out of the cedar grove.

As he did so, two things immediately claimed his attention. South of him smoke was rising. Campfire, he thought. To the northwest, clouds of dust billowed in the air. Riders, he thought.

Both the smoke and the dust made him uneasy. Both raised questions in his mind. Whose campfire had he spotted? Who were the invisible riders hidden in the swirling dust?

The answers to his questions were important at any time for a man riding alone almost anywhere, but here, in Indian Territory, he knew the answers were of major importance.

He rode back the way he had come and in among the cedars again. He watched the rising dust almost without blinking until he was able to make out the half-hidden figure of a man in the midst of it. Then, another. Both men, he saw a moment later, were wearing cavalry uniforms and out of the dust behind them appeared other figures. Indians. The men mounted, the women on foot. All of them flanked by troopers, twelve in all.

He glanced south. No sign of smoke now. He left the protection of the trees and rode toward the cavalry's long line that was moving slowly in the dust that hovered above the guards and the guarded alike.

When he reached the haggard officer with the rugged face who was leading the long column, he nodded a greeting. "Bound for the Darlington Indian Agency, are you, Lieutenant?"

"We are, sir."

"Cheyennes?" Cimarron asked, pointing to the Indians.

11

"Northern Cheyennes, yes. Major Linnett, the Fourth Cavalry's commanding officer at Fort Reno, sent us out to gather them up. It's been a long journey and they're tired. It's time we stopped to rest." The lieutenant turned in his saddle and spoke to the man riding behind him. "Sergeant, we'll halt here for a brief respite. See that our men and the Indians have enough water."

"Lieutenant, my name's Cimarron. I'm a deputy marshal out of Fort Smith and I'm hunting a horse thief by the name of Jake Farley. Did you happen to spot a lone rider heading west?"

"I did not," the lieutenant replied as he and Cimarron dismounted. "I'm Lieutenant Henry Kendrick." He held out his hand and Cimarron shook it. "You're something of a rarity, I must say, Cimarron."

"Me?"

"I've never seen a marshal out here before."

"Deputy marshal."

"From what I've been told, deputy marshals are seldom seen west of the Katy railroad."

"Some of us do get farther west than that from time to time. Me for one." Cimarron watched the Indians as they stood or sat in silence. "They're a woebegone bunch if I ever saw one."

"It's been a long march for them. They were settled on the Red Cloud Agency up in Nebraska until someone in Washington, apparently in conjunction with the central superintendency in Lawrence, Kansas, decided they should be moved down here to the Cheyenne-Arapaho reservation."

"Those politicians, whether they happen to be back in Washington or up in Kansas, got themselves more ideas of what to do with these Indians than a dog has fleas."

"More is the pity," Kendrick commented.

"I take it you don't exactly relish marching them all over hell's half-acre."

"It is my duty. I do it." Kendrick glanced at the Cheyennes, all of them still silent and expressionless, and grimaced. "Most of them didn't want to come south. But they finally agreed to do so. They really had precious little choice in the matter and they knew it. If you ask me, it's an injudicious decision, whoever made it. These northerners never did get along all that well with the southern Cheyennes and now, with so many southerners already on the reservation down here, well, there's bound to be friction if not outright trouble of one sort or another."

"You called me a rarity before, Kendrick. Seems to me you're one yourself."

Kendrick's eyebrows arched questioningly.

"You're a pony soldier who's clearly got some sympathy for the Indians. Most troopers I've known in my time were either scared shitless of Indians or they wanted to kill as many of them as quick as they could."

"I've killed Indians," Kendrick said slowly. "I am not boasting. I am merely stating a fact. I've fought the Plains tribes more times than I like to remember. But that was war. This—" Kendrick waved a hand toward the Cheyennes, "this is—well, it is not the kind of duty I prefer."

"Some of those writers in the eastern papers, they'd most likely call it shameful."

When Kendrick said nothing, Cimarron studied the Indians gathered in the distance. The men avoided his eyes as the women busied themselves with their babies and the packs strapped to the countless dogs among the group. He began to feel uncomfortable as he always did in the presence of men who would not meet his eyes. Such men, he had long ago learned, were either dangerous or, as in the case of these Cheyenne braves, beaten.

"So you didn't see the man I'm trailing," he said finally, looking away from the Indians and back at Kendrick.

"I'm afraid not. He must be a very dangerous man for you to have come this far west looking for him."

"Jake Farley's not all that dangerous. Shifty, yes. Sly, yes. But no more dangerous than a sidewinder when you've got a big stick and some clout. I almost had him west of Wewoka but he gave me the slip. Well, Kendrick, I'd best be moseying along after him. It was a pleasure meeting up with you. Haven't had anybody to talk to in so long my tongue's turned rusty."

"Good luck, Cimarron. I hope you apprehend your man."

"I'll get him," Cimarron said as he stepped into the saddle and then, with a wave to Kendrick, rode west.

How long had it been, he asked himself. Days. He really wasn't sure exactly how many. But he was sure that he had used his tongue for more than talking when he had last met someone on the plains.

She had told him her name was Carrie. She was, she said, driving her team and wagon north to Tulsey Town in Creek Nation for supplies.

He had told her that was a coincidence, since he happened to be heading in the same direction, which was a lie because he was heading southwest. But she had been pretty. Young and pretty and she never seemed to stop smiling at him and he felt warmed and encouraged by her smiles and he almost whooped with delight when it began to rain and there was no shelter in sight on the plain.

They took cover under a tarpaulin in the bed of her spring wagon and, as the rain spattered it, they talked a little at first and then they touched a lot and before long he was on top of her and she was moaning with pleasure.

Cimarron, remembering Carrie now as he rode along, smiled to himself. He never did learn her last name, not that it mattered. But he had learned other things about her. He had learned that she was both passionate and, once she had gotten used to being where she was with him, uninhibited.

It's a wonder, he thought, that it ever got soft again on me considering the way she carried on with her teeth and her hot hands and her hotter tongue that she knew more ways to use on me than any other woman I ever had.

He glanced to the right. Kendrick had said he hadn't seen any lone rider. So it was likely that Farley was still heading west although there was no way to be certain of that. He looked to the south and saw only the empty plain in that direction. Remembering the campfire smoke he had seen earlier when the cavalry came into sight, he looked back over his shoulder.

A rider. In the distance and coming toward him.

He drew rein and sat his saddle, watching the rider approach, his right hand resting on the butt of his Colt. He was surprised when the rider suddenly turned north. He continued watching until both horse and rider disappeared among the trees that were growing along the river.

Something's not right, he thought. Something's wrong. A rider doesn't ride in one direction and then up and change direction for no good reason I can spot.

Am I being trailed, he wondered. Or am I just getting

14

spooked out here with a horse thief somewhere up ahead of me and somebody I don't know riding behind me?

He turned the bay and continued riding west, looking back over his shoulder from time to time but seeing no one behind him. Could the rider have been Jake Farley? Had the man doubled back and then come up behind me? This job I've got is getting to me, he thought. It's turning me as skittish as a bronc that's wearing a saddle for the first time. The rider was probably heading for the reservation, he decided. An Indian maybe. Probably. An Indian that got a sudden notion to turn north away from the reservation? His explanation made little sense and he knew it.

When he came to a dry wash, he rode down into it after a speculative glance in the direction of the timbered region to the north. He halted his horse and got out of the saddle. He waited a moment and then climbed up the low bank on his right. Taking off his hat, he peered over the edge of the bank. He saw only the trees near the river. He looked back over his shoulder and saw only the plain, which was littered in places with boulders. He clapped his hat back on his head and then slid down the bank. Taking the reins in one hand, he led his horse to the western end of the wash. He walked up its slight incline and then, when he saw nothing ahead of him—

But there was something ahead of him. In a grassless stretch of ground in the distance he saw the hoof prints. Three sharp. One blurred.

Farley.

He swung into the saddle and spurred the bay. As it came racing out of the wash, a shot rang out.

He turned the bay with one sharp tug on the reins and as the horse galloped back down into the wash, he leaped from the saddle after drawing his Winchester from the boot. The bay ran on and then stopped, swinging its head around to look back at him.

He flattened his body against the sloping side of the wash and then scrambled up it to peer at the trees in the north. That rider I spotted, he told himself, must be holed up in those woods. He braced the barrel of his rifle on the level ground and sighted along it, waiting for the next shot from whoever it was who was trying to take him.

When the shot he had been expecting did come, it took him by surprise because it came not from the trees but from behind him. Instantly, he slid down into the wash and then quickly scrambled up the other side to peer south, the direction from which the second shot had come.

You're a damn fool, he told himself angrily. You spot a rider heading north. You see trees in the north. You get yourself shot at. You figure the rider did the shooting from the trees. Damn fool, you jump to conclusions quicker'n some men jump another's claim.

The boulders.

His gaze darted from one to the next and on to the next. Any one of them was large enough for a bushwhacker to hide behind. One pile was almost as big as a battlement.

Minutes passed.

He decided to try to provoke some action. He squeezed off a shot and chips of stone were torn from the nearest boulder.

A man's head and arms suddenly appeared above a more distant boulder. He raised a rifle and fired.

Cimarron fired simultaneously and the man ducked down out of sight—the man he had recognized as Jake Farley.

Farley must have decided to wait for him, he thought. He must have decided to put an end to me and my trailing. Now how the hell am I going to take him alive? If I go and kill him, I won't get paid my two dollars for bringing him in. What's worse, I'll have to bury the bastard.

His thoughts were dispersed as Farley, crouching, ran forward and then dropped down behind a boulder closer to the wash.

Cimarron got off another shot at his quarry, which went wild as the dry ground beneath his boots crumbled and he slid part way down the bank.

He was up again and aiming almost at once, bracing his boots in holes he had toed into the bank.

No sign of Farley.

Got to do something, he thought. Got to flush Farley out without getting a hole in my hide in the process. He scrambled down the side of the wash and went running back through it. He hesitated a moment at its mouth and then came up shooting and running for the boulder closest to him.

Farley got off a shot as Cimarron dived behind the boulder, but the shot missed.

Close though, Cimarron thought. The jasper's almost as good with a rifle as he is at stealing horses. He got to his

16

knees and peered around the side of the boulder he was crouching behind. Still no good. Farley had circled his boulder and remained out of sight.

Cimarron swore.

There was another broken mass of boulders to his left. Not a very high mound, he realized, but high enough for a man bellying down on the ground to hide behind. He'd be taking a risk if he came out into the open again. But it might be worth it.

Farley rose and fired again. His shot struck the boulder behind which Cimarron crouched. As the sound of the shot died away, Cimarron heard another sound, a distant one. He pressed his ear to the ground and covered his other ear with his free left hand. A horse. Coming this way. He straightened and looked around but saw no horse.

As Farley rose from behind his boulder, Cimarron fired at him before he could squeeze the trigger. Farley dropped down without firing.

Hoofbeats sounded. Closer now.

Cimarron eased around the boulder. There it was! The horse he had heard galloping. Horse and rider were coming from the northeast. He recognized the horse as the one he had seen earlier coming up behind him.

His gaze darted from the horse and rider to the boulder behind which Farley remained invisible. Now what exactly is going on here, he asked himself. Who's that rider after? Farley? Or me?

He saw the rifle in the rider's hand rise and he ducked down as a shot blazed from it.

Somebody let out a yell.

The rider? Farley?

Cimarron heard another shot. He peered around the boulder and saw that Farley was up and running.

Well now, he thought as he stood up, took aim, and fired at Farley, who kept on running.

A moment later, Farley darted behind the low battlement and then he reappeared aboard a horse and went galloping north.

Cimarron raced back to the wash. He jumped down into it and climbed quickly into the saddle. He spurred the bay and a moment later, as he came out of the wash, he went riding north after Farley.

"Cimarron!"

He turned in the saddle and looked back in surprise at the mounted rider he now realized was a woman.

"Cimarron!" she shouted again and gestured wildly. *"Stop!"*

He drew rein, turned the bay, and headed back toward the woman he was sure he had never seen before in his life but who seemed, in some strange way, familiar to him. As he drew abreast of her, he came to a halt. "You know me?"

"Now what kind of question is that?"

"Sensible kind, seems to me."

"After what I just did for you don't tell me that you have the unmitigated gall not to thank me for it?"

"Just what is it you figure you just did for me?"

"Why—why—" she spluttered and pointed.

Cimarron stared at the retreating figure of Farley and watched as the man disappeared in the trees.

"I drove him off, that's what I did for you!" the woman cried. "I may have saved your life!"

He studied her. Slim figure but noticeable hips and even more noticeable breasts. Deep cleavage visible because the top buttons of the man's shirt she was wearing were unbuttoned. Her jeans were dusty and her boots scuffed. She's done some traveling, he thought.

"I'm almost sorry I did!" she cried in exasperation.

"Did what?"

"Save your life!"

"What you did is you went and run off the man I was after."

She had smooth skin which was naturally dark and darkened still further by the sun. Indian, Cimarron thought. Full-blood. Her nose was straight and so was the line of her lips. Her eyes were inky and her hair, unbound and hanging well below her shoulders, was as black.

She pushed her Stetson back on her head and booted her Spencer carbine.

"How come you know my name?" Cimarron asked her.

"Oh, I know quite a good deal about you, not just your name. I know, for example, that you're a deputy marshal and I know how you got that scar on the left side of your face. You were helping your father brand cattle when you were a boy and accidentally let a calf get away

18

from you. Your father became angry and swung the red-hot branding iron he had in his hand. It raked your face."

"How do you know how I got my scar?"

"Do you remember a woman named Alma Ralston?"

"Alma Ralston," Cimarron repeated thoughtfully, and a moment later his eyes lit up. "Why, sure I do. I met her down in Tishomingo in Chickasaw Nation."

"Well, I can tell you, she hasn't forgotten you or your ways."

"Is that a fact? Alma and me, we had us some good times together." Cimarron paused, remembering. "But how'd you recognize me? By my scar? Or did Alma describe me to you?"

"The picnic."

"What picnic?"

"Alma would be very sorry to hear that you've forgotten the picnic you and she attended at which a photographer took a picture of the two of you together. She showed me the picture, which she sets great store by."

Cimarron recalled the picnic on the bank of the Washita River as the woman's eyes left his face and roamed down his body. "Who are you?" he asked her.

"My name is Beatrice and I'm still waiting."

"What're you waiting for, Beatrice?"

"For a word of thanks for what I just did for you."

"I thought I made it clear to you. You didn't do me any favor. More like a disservice, to tell the truth. Now I'll have to ride out and try my best to find Farley again and who knows where he might be by now?"

"I'm sure you'll find him if that is what you are still intent on doing."

"Well, what else would I be intent on doing? Finding Jake Farley's my job. You said you knew I was a deputy marshal so—"

"You make me feel as if I owe you an apology for what I did—for trying to help you."

"I spotted the smoke of your campfire. Then I spotted you. Tell me something. How come you headed north once you knew I'd seen you?"

Beatrice lowered her head a moment and then looked up, avoiding Cimarron's eyes. "I had to answer a call of nature and I wanted to do it privately, not with you watching me,

19

so I rode for the trees growing along the river." She reached up and buttoned her shirt to the neck.

Cimarron immediately decided he was going about matters the wrong way. It was time to change course. "How is Alma Ralston? I mean the last time you saw her, how was she?"

"Oh, she's fine. She confessed to me that she still pines for you and, now that I've met you, I can, I think, understand why."

"She sure was a good—" Cimarron managed to suppress the bawdy word he had been about to utter and concluded, "friend."

"A man like you must have, I suppose, a goodly number of women friends."

"I have a few." An image of Carrie flitted through his mind although he wasn't at all sure that she could qualify as a friend. He was sure though that she could qualify as an interesting acquaintance. He decided to give Beatrice what she wanted. "Thank you for keeping Farley from drilling me."

"You're welcome."

"It's good you showed up when you did. You were about as welcome as ice in hell," he lied.

"I was on my way to visit my father when I heard that man you called Farley fire on you. I felt I had to help and then later, when you came close to me, I recognized you. Isn't it a small world?"

"You're traveling all alone?"

"Yes. As I said, I'm on my way to my father. He's a cattle rancher north of here in the Unassigned Lands." Beatrice patted the stock of her Spencer. "I can take quite good care of myself."

"I believe you can. Well, I'd best be riding out after Farley. Since you're heading north and so is Farley, you and me we could ride along together if you've no objection."

"I'd like that."

"Me too. I might just have need of you in case I find Farley and he starts shooting at me again."

Beatrice laughed. "I'm really not as brave as I pretended to be a moment ago," she confided. "So I might have need of you. As Alma told me she did," she added.

Cimarron, as he and Beatrice rode north, wondered what she had meant by her last remark. Had she been referring to the fact that he had run off the man who had been harassing Alma when they met? Or was she referring to the other needs of Alma's which he had met later?

He noticed that Beatrice was opening the top buttons of her shirt.

"It's hot, isn't it?" she asked without looking at him.

"I am," he answered and, when she glanced at him, an unreadable expression on her face, he gave her a big grin.

2

They rode north side by side without speaking and later, as they forded the north fork of the Canadian River, they were still silent.

Cimarron tried to think of something to say but nothing came to him, at least nothing he dared say out loud to this woman he was riding with and who seemed to be lost in thought. He studied the ground around him as he rode, searching for sign of Farley but he found none.

The land over which they traveled was level and without much cover, which bothered him. He and his companion, he was aware, made easy targets out here on the open plain. He took consolation from the fact that Farley too would be a highly visible and easy target. But there were places a man could hide even here. All he needed was some tall grass or a rain-eroded gully in the ground.

He kept his eyes moving, first to the left, then to the right, then up ahead. There was no one in sight. He glanced over his shoulder. No one behind him. His uneasiness increased as he thought about Farley, trying to guess what his quarry's next move might turn out to be. Headlong flight? Or would Farley decide to lie in wait in some suitable spot as he had done before? Would he double back? Cimarron knew that Farley was not the kind of man who would reject the idea of shooting an unsuspecting man in the back. The thought only added to his uneasiness.

He glanced covertly at Beatrice, who was staring straight ahead. His shadow fell on her and the horse she was riding. Her shadow and that of her horse stretched out beyond them. Sun's setting soon, he thought. Better scout a place to spend the night. He forgot Farley momentarily as he thought about the night that was coming and what it might hold for him. For him and Beatrice.

Better start warming her up. How? "You don't live with your daddy on his ranch?" he asked.

"No," she replied. "My brother and I remained behind in Creek Nation when he decided to come here to try his hand at cattle ranching."

"You come from a big family?"

"No. There were just the four of us. There are only two of us now. My mother died when my brother and I were quite young. He died two years ago."

"I'm sorry to hear that."

Beatrice looked at him and then away. "I'm used to living alone."

It was a statement made with both pride and a trace of ferocity, Cimarron noted. "You never got married?"

"No. There was a man—" She didn't finish what she had started to say.

"I've no doubt there was," Cimarron said. "A comely woman like yourself would be bound to have a man. Even if she didn't want one, she'd be bound to have one. At least one. Probably lots more. I can see them now. Prowling restless and eager around you, struck next to senseless by those big black eyes of yours and that soft long hair, that smooth skin you've got, your figure—" His words trailed away.

"We were to have been married," Beatrice said as if she had been paying no attention to Cimarron's remarks, "but life changes people's plans. Sometimes a person sets out in one direction and then finds himself traveling in quite another as a result of events he had not anticipated nor could he have changed however hard he might have tried to change them."

"That's the truth," Cimarron agreed, noticing the burned grass off to his left where someone had built a fire. Farley? "It's happened to me like that," he added.

"We Creeks," Beatrice said, "have a capacity for endurance. We survived, most of us, the persecution of the whites in the East and then the terrible trek west. Many of us not only survived but have prospered. We have within us—perhaps it's born in us or maybe it's a matter of our Creek blood—the capacity to persevere and even triumph as we set about reaching the goals we set for ourselves."

24

Cimarron barely heard what Beatrice said because he was traveling along another trail and he was alone upon it. It led him and the other outlaws he was riding with at the time those many years ago to a small town in Texas and then to the bank in that town.

He was inside the bank now as he had been then. He was kneeling in front of the open door of the heavy iron safe and he was stuffing money he took from the safe into a sack. And then—from the door came a shout.

He whirled, gun in hand, and fired at the sheriff who had shouted and was standing, pistol drawn, in the doorway. The man blocked the sun that had been streaming through the door. But the sun returned as the sheriff went down, Cimarron's bullet in his heart.

He was up and running fast then but, a split second after passing the sheriff he had killed, he halted, turned . . .

And recognized the man he had killed as the man who had sired him. Shock shook him. The gun that was still in his hand quivered because his hand was trembling.

He heard himself asking questions of the terrified patrons in the bank and he heard their answers. The man had come to their town years earlier following the death of his wife. They had come to know and respect him. They had asked him, a decent and law-abiding man, to be their sheriff. He had consented.

Cimarron went running out of the bank. He tossed the sack of money to one of his companions and then boarded his horse. He rode away alone and remained, even when with others, alone in the haunted years that followed.

Behind him rode the memory of the man who had been his father. That memory stalked him while he was awake and when he was drowning in dreams. It asked him why. He had never been able to answer the question. He had been able only to ride on, trying desperately but hopelessly to put enough distance between himself and the memory so that he might one day, one longed-for and blessed day, be able to erase the memory and end the pain it almost constantly caused him.

"Is something wrong, Cimarron?"

He lurched back into the present where the sun was below the horizon now and Beatrice was staring at him with a puzzled expression on her face.

"Nope," he answered. "I'm fine." A lie. He felt far from fine.

"Hadn't we better find some place to spend the night?"

"I'd like very much to spend the night with you, Beatrice," Cimarron said, "but I'd best keep after Farley."

"It will soon be dark."

"It will. But till it is, I can keep after him. Even when it does get dark, maybe I can spot a fire if he's foolish enough to build one out in the open."

"I wish you wouldn't go," Beatrice said softly.

Cimarron studied her face. He really didn't want to leave her. He wanted . . . Did she know what he wanted? He suspected she did.

Did she want it too?

"It's a bit out of our way but I figure we ought to head west," he said.

"Then you'll stay the night with me?"

Cimarron nodded, the trace of a smile on his face.

"Why do you think we should head west?"

"There's shelter there."

"Timber?"

"Hills. Let's head for them." He turned his horse to the left and rode west.

Beatrice followed him and later, as they rode in among the sloping hills that were capped with thick layers of white gypsum glowing orange in the light of the setting sun, Cimarron chose a spot between two hills where some scrub oak grew for their camp. Before dismounting, he checked the wind direction and then, once on the ground, he led his bay to a patch of ground that was thick with edible forbs and picketed it so that it could graze against the wind as horses usually preferred to do in warm weather.

He hobbled the animal, stripped his gear from it, spread his blanket on the ground to air, and dropped his saddle and bridle beside it. He beckoned to Beatrice and he soon had her horse picketed near his own and her gear lying on the ground beside his. Then, after gathering some dry wood that was lying on the ground beneath the oaks, he built a fire.

"Aren't you afraid someone might see our fire?" Beatrice asked him.

"I plan on keeping it low. It's to keep coyotes and maybe

wolves at a distance, not to cook over. Truth is, I got nothing at all to cook.''

"I have some pemmican in my parfleche. Some jerky too. I'll be happy to share it with you."

"We'll share and share alike, how about that? I've got some dried corn I've been splitting between me and that bay of mine but I'd much rather split it with you seeing as how my horse has good grass and clover to graze over there."

"Those horses seem contented, don't they? I stopped for a rest around noon the day before yesterday and my horse just would not stop fidgeting. I guess he was hot."

"You stop in timber or out in the open?"

"In timber."

"That tells the tale. Horses spot shadows when the sun's shining through woods and they get spooked."

"You know a lot about animals it seems."

"Know a thing or two about people too. A man like me learns a bit if he keeps his eyes and ears open while he wanders. A lot of what he learns comes in real handy from time to time."

Cimarron went over to the horses and, using handfuls of grass, carefully rubbed both of them down until there was no sign of sweat on either of their bodies. He stood beside them, gazing out at the plain from between the sheltering hills, wondering where Farley was making camp for the night that lay ahead.

He was a tall man and a lean one and, as he stood there, the sun's final faint glow illuminated his face and the scar on it that ran from just below his left eye down over his cheek to stop just above the corner of his mouth. It was a raised ridge of dead flesh that even the day's last light could not bring to life. After pushing his black slouch hat back on his head, he hooked his thumbs in the leather cartridge belt he wore around his slender hips. He stood at ease but alert, his heavily muscled body not entirely relaxed but ready, should the need arise, to swing swiftly into action. The bony fingers of his strong hands were motionless as they rested lightly against his thighs.

He had thin lips beneath an equally thin but wide-nostriled nose. His cheeks were slightly sunken and his emerald eyes set deep beneath an overhanging brow. He continued speculating about Farley's whereabouts but he was aware that his thoughts of his quarry were being shouldered aside by intruding thoughts of Beatrice. His right hand rose and removed his hat. He ran the fingers of his left hand through his straight black hair, which buried both of his ears and the nape of his neck.

What was there about Beatrice? Something. Something vaguely familiar. Had he ever met her? He doubted it. For two reasons. If he had met her, he would have remembered such a desirable woman and also, if he had, she would undoubtedly have reminded him of their meeting, but she had done no such thing. Still there was something about her that struck a faint chord in his memory. He shifted position slightly so that she was within his line of vision and clapped his hat back on his head.

He watched her remove a parfleche from her saddlebag. He was sure they had never met, so he must be thinking of some other woman who resembled her. But the only other Creek woman he knew well was Sarah Lassiter. He smiled to himself. But Sarah, that sweet woman, had been smaller than Beatrice. Her figure had been almost girlish while Beatrice had the ripe and strongly appealing figure of a grown woman.

"Cimarron," she called to him. "Shall we eat now?"

He nodded and walked toward her as the day's light disappeared and shadows quickly shrouded the open area between the surrounding hills, leaving only the light of the fire to faintly brighten the young night.

After sharing their provisions, they began to eat, both of them seated on the ground in front of the fire.

Cimarron chewed a mouthful of dried corn, swallowed it, and asked, "You and me, we've never met before, have we?"

Beatrice shook her head and then, smiling, said, "I'm sure I would have remembered meeting you."

"Thanks for the compliment, if that's what it was. I asked because I can't help feeling there's something familiar about you."

"I'm not unlike a lot of other women in face or figure. I imagine you've met so many women that perhaps we all begin to look alike to you."

Cimarron bit off a piece of jerky from the strip he held in his hand. "You do tend to stand out from the rest."

"Thank you for the compliment. If that's what it was." Beatrice rose, got her bedroll, and spread it out not far from the fire. "I'm tired. You'll excuse me, Cimarron?"

"Sure I will. I'm feeling weary myself." He ate the last of his jerky and then made his bed not far from where Beatrice was lying. Beside it, he placed his rifle and revolver and then, after a moment's hesitation, added Beatrice's rifle to his cache of arms. He pulled off his boots and then removed his hat and cartridge belt. He lay down, wrapping his blanket around him. "Night's getting chilly," he observed.

No response.

"I could do with another blanket. Something to keep me warm. You asleep already?"

No response.

He propped his head up on one elbow and stared at Beatrice, who was facing away from him. He moved closer to her, sliding the tarpaulin beneath him and dragging his blanket along. He put an arm around her.

"Alma was right," she said.

"She was? What about?"

"You. She said that she believed you must spend more than half of your life with your jeans down and your—you know—up."

"My jeans are still on but my—you know—it's all the way up on account of you."

Beatrice's hand slid under Cimarron's blanket and, as she fumbled with the buttons of his jeans, he shifted position so that she could undo them more easily. He felt her begin to tug on his jeans so he arched his body helpfully. As Beatrice slid his jeans down over his hips, he snapped erect.

"Alma was right about one or two other things too," she whispered, moving closer to him. "She said you were bigger than any man she'd ever known before. Your—it's almost alarming."

"Honey, it needn't be. Fact of the matter is, big as it is, it can be a genuine consolation to a real woman like yourself."

Beatrice stroked him lightly and then gripped him fiercely. "I'm not sure—I'm tight, or so I've been told."

"That's no drawback, not for either of us it isn't," he assured her as he throbbed in her warm hand that was still holding him tightly. "Me being big and you being tight works in our favor. We're certain to be able to pleasure each

29

other just fine because of how we're both built." He took her head in both hands and kissed her on the lips.

She released her hold on him and snuggled closer to him.

As he continued to kiss her, Cimarron kicked his legs and was finally free of his jeans. He withdrew his lips and began to unbutton Beatrice's shirt. He opened it wide and bent his head. As he sucked the nipples of her breasts, one after the other, he felt her move so that she was lying on her back.

"That's it," he said. "Make yourself comfortable." He began to unbutton her jeans. When he pulled them off he tossed them to one side and eased himself down on her so that his erection was cradled between her thighs.

"Will it—it's going to hurt me, I know it is," Beatrice breathed. Her hands rose and her palms pressed against Cimarron's chest.

"We'll take it slow. Bit by bit. You will, I mean. Like this." He barely penetrated her, remained immobile a moment, then withdrew.

He waited a moment during which he kissed her again, this time forcing his tongue between her teeth, and then he pressed himself against her and on into her, farther this time. He drew back without leaving her, his tongue exploring her mouth, and he lowered his hips when her hands left his chest.

He felt her moistness that soon became wetness and he penetrated her more deeply. Her arms went around him as their lips parted.

"That's all of it?" she murmured.

"Almost. Now, don't you fret. You're doing just fine." He fondled her left breast with his right hand. This time, when he thrust his tongue between her teeth, she began to suck it. He held himself steady as she worked on his tongue and then, slowly, he eased all the way into her.

She gave a wordless moan and pulled her head to one side. Then her hips rose as if she were trying to engulf him completely.

Cimarron thrust down hard this time and, a moment later, their bodies were pounding rhythmically and he was trying hard not to let himself go, not yet.

Beneath him, Beatrice bit her lower lip. Her legs rose and encircled his thighs.

He suddenly withdrew from her and she let out a cry of

what might have been anguish. In response to it, he plunged back into her with sudden force and began to buck.

When her nails bit into his buttocks, he moaned and, sweating, erupted, his body shuddering and his toes curling.

Beatrice tightened her grip on him as she too shuddered, her breath coming in rapid gusts and her chest heaving.

"I feel flooded," she murmured, and sighed deeply.

Cimarron, his cheek against hers, remained with her, still erect, feeling his ecstasy begin to settle into satisfaction.

"I feel," Beatrice said almost inaudibly, "as if I could stay like this forever."

He nibbled her ear lobe.

She shivered beneath him. Her lips parted.

His pressed against hers and she eagerly took his tongue. He relaxed on top of her and let her have her way with it for a time. Then he withdrew from her and flopped down on his back. He drew the blankets over himself and Beatrice and fumbled for her hand beneath them. When he found it, he squeezed it lightly.

Her other hand moved along his chest, caressed his nipples until they stiffened, and then her hand moved down over his navel to grip his slowly softening flesh.

He became hard again almost immediately and, as her index finger delicately massaged the underside of his erection, he felt himself beginning to soar once again. He was about to speak but, before he could do so, he exploded, drenching the blanket and Beatrice's hand.

"Oh!" she cried. "Cimarron, I'm sorry! I didn't mean to—I didn't know you could—so soon, I mean. I'm amazed!"

He heaved a sigh of contentment. "There's not a need in the whole wide world for you to be sorry, honey. What you did just then was close to as good as what we both did before." He kissed her lightly and then composed himself for sleep.

He heard her stirring beside him and he found the sounds she was making comforting. For a man like me who's too much alone, he thought, having her nearby's a real pleasure. Hell, he thought, I won't even mind if she snores.

She didn't. But she did cause him to snap awake, every sense instantly alert, in the deep darkness some untold time later. His hand swiftly closed on his Colt but the rest of his body remained motionless as he watched her moving about in

31

the dull glow of the few flames left in the fire. Was she about to answer another of nature's calls, as she had put it to him earlier when he had questioned her about her movements on the trail? No. She seemed to be searching for something.

"You hunting for your Spencer?" he asked her.

"Oh," she said, turning quickly toward him. "You startled me. No, I was—I couldn't sleep. I was too excited to sleep. I'm sorry I woke you."

"You'd best get back here if you don't want to find yourself sitting asleep in the saddle tomorrow."

She returned and lay down beside him.

"I've got your rifle right here," he told her.

She yawned and turned over without saying anything more.

Cimarron listened to her quiet breathing and then he too let himself slip into sleep.

After a quick meal of jerky and pemmican early the next morning, they got their horses ready to ride and then left their camp of the night before.

They rode northeast and then due north, Cimarron searching the ground for sign of Farley, Beatrice giving him occasional surreptitious glances that he pretended not to notice.

"You'll find him," she said finally, as if she thought he needed encouragement. "I know you will."

"I'm trying to. But so far—no luck."

They rode on and they had covered, Cimarron estimated, a good four or five miles when he heard Beatrice gasp.

"They're not hunting us," he told her, referring to the Indians he had spotted in the distance before she had done so. "They're probably out here hunting buffalo. My guess is they're from the Cheyenne-Arapaho reservation due west of us."

He became aware of the fact that she had, either deliberately or accidentally, moved her horse closer to his bay. "They don't look bent on harm," he said in an effort to reassure her, aware that her body had tensed as she continued to stare straight ahead of her at the Indians. "Half of them don't even have guns of any kind."

"The arrows they have can kill," Beatrice observed. "Their lances can too."

He watched as the Indians, mounted and accompanied by a string of packhorses, moved north ahead of them.

"Couldn't we stop?" Beatrice asked him uneasily. "Just until those Indians are gone?"

"We could. But we're not going to. I want to have a talk with those hunters. Come on." He spurred his bay and began to gallop toward the Indians. When he reached them, he realized that Beatrice had remained behind. He saw her still sitting on her horse where he had left her.

The Indians had halted and were staring silently at Cimarron.

He swept his right hand across his brow in the sign for white man and then moved a finger up from his lips in the sign for friend. He pointed to the brave nearest to him who wore only leggings and moccasins and then he made a sweeping motion with his right hand to include the entire band of braves.

An Indian rode up beside the one Cimarron had addressed and held a hand near his mouth. The first two fingers of his hand were extended, the others folded out of sight.

"I'm not double-tongued," Cimarron said hotly, exasperated. "I'm not lying. I'm your friend—or will be, if you'll let me."

He raised both hands and placed them on either side of his head, his index fingers pointing to the sky in the sign for buffalo. Then he pantomimed drawing a bow.

Both Indians nodded.

Again he swept his hand across his brow, repeating the sign for white man, and then pointed to his eyes and then in several different directions, swiveling his head as if he were searching for something.

"We saw a white man," said the brave he had first addressed.

"Now, why didn't you tell me you could talk English?" Shaking his head, Cimarron described Farley to the Indian who had spoken and who replied, "We saw him."

He started to form new signs and then, remembering that he could be understood in English, instead asked, "Which way was he headed?"

The brave pointed west.

"How long ago did you see him?" When neither Indian responded, Cimarron pointed to the sun, then to the east, and then made the sign for darkness.

"The sun was rising when we saw white man," the brave said. "Who are you?"

Cimarron identified himself and showed the brave his badge, which he pulled from the pocket of his jeans.

The brave touched his chest. "War Pony." He pointed to the Indian beside him. "Nine Fingers. We are Northern Cheyennes." He moved a finger up from his lips in the sign for friend which was based on the motion a man made when smoking a peace pipe. He pointed to Nine Fingers.

"Much obliged, War Pony," Cimarron said. "West, you said." He looked in that direction and then back at Beatrice. He beckoned to her and she quirted her horse and rode toward him, anxiety etched on her features.

"You bring your woman on hunt?" War Pony asked him.

"One of you, I noticed, brought yours," Cimarron countered and pointed to the mounted woman behind War Pony who was wearing a buckskin tunic and leggings and whose braids were unadorned.

"She is no man's woman," War Pony said, and Cimarron thought he detected a note of pride in the tone. "She is Warrior Woman."

War Pony's remarks explained nothing to Cimarron. He decided to pursue the matter no further.

One of the Indians let out a yell and, as he did, Beatrice cried out in alarm.

"It's all right," Cimarron told her. "Get a grip on yourself."

War Pony dug his heels into the sides of his pony and went galloping east, the other braves and Warrior Woman riding close behind him.

"Buffalo," Cimarron explained to Beatrice. He pointed to where a small herd of eight buffaloes were rounding a stand of post oaks and moving out onto the plain.

"They're going to kill them?" she asked.

"Sure, they are. They'll eat the meat, make lodge coverings with the hides, sun dance altars out of the skulls, leggings and mittens for winter—all sorts and manner of things. The buffalo's their commissary and general store all rolled up into one and set down on four short legs."

He watched the Indians split into two separate columns. The surround began as the two columns gradually converged at a gallop on the herd, the Indians shrieking and waving their arms to turn the lead bull back into the herd.

Once the bull had been turned and the five cows and the other two bulls began to swirl in their confusion and fear, the Indians fired their arrows and threw their lances. The buffaloes bellowed in pain and rage as thick clouds of dust rose around them. They continued to circle aimlessly, partially blinded now by the dust, desperately lashing out with their horns.

War Pony's horse was gored out from under him. As the animal went down, some of its internal organs slipping through the gash in its side, War Pony leaped to his feet and hurled his lance, which buried itself in a cow's shoulder. The cow ran on until Warrior Woman's lance downed her.

One of the bulls was felled by Nine Fingers and another Cheyenne. Two cows made a run for it and were promptly pursued by several Cheyennes. Moments later, the cows were on the ground, their bodies shuddering in their death agony.

Cimarron, still watching, suddenly tensed in his saddle. "War Pony!" he yelled at the top of his voice, his hands cupped around his mouth.

But War Pony didn't respond. He continued stalking one of the remaining cows on foot as the lead bull, shaking its head and lowering its horns, pawed the ground not far behind him.

Cimarron jerked his Winchester from the boot and then rode to the north. He halted the bay, raised his rifle, and fired. His shot entered the bull's shoulder from behind as the animal made a dash at War Pony who turned, saw the still-charging bull, and swiftly leaped to one side.

Cimarron fired a second time and this time the bull dropped to its knees, its head sagging.

War Pony looked down at the dead bull and then at Cimarron. He seized the rope bridle of a riderless horse and leaped on its back.

When he reached Cimarron, he said, "You did well."

Cimarron nodded.

"Come. You will share in the kill." Without waiting for a response, he rode back to the dead buffaloes among which his fellow hunters were scurrying, their knife blades glinting in the light of the sun.

"You're not going, are you?" Beatrice asked Cimarron.

"Sure I am. Wouldn't be polite not to go now that I've been invited."

He rode out with Beatrice slowly following him and, when he reached the scene of the slaughter, he dismounted, pulled his knife from his boot and began to skin a dead cow, aware that War Pony was surreptitiously watching him.

When he had finished his task, his hands and forearms were as bloody as his knife.

War Pony shouted orders in his own language and Nine Fingers, Warrior Woman, and the other hunters began to load meat on their pack horses. He bent down to the carcass at his feet and thrust a hand into it. His hand emerged holding a tangle of intestines which he severed and then walked toward Cimarron. He held the intestines out and Cimarron took them from him.

"Eat," he said. "The intestines—the brains. Won't keep."

Cimarron's teeth tore into the slimy mass in his hand as War Pony looked on approvingly and Beatrice began to retch.

Cimarron continued to eat, ignoring Beatrice, and apparently ignored by War Pony who moved among the hunters as they carved up their kill, which they had identified by the painted markings on their arrows and lances.

Cimarron dropped what remained of the intestines War Pony had given him on the ground and then bent down and cut the heart out of the buffalo carcass lying at his feet. He tossed it to the ground.

"Aren't you going to eat that heart too?" Beatrice asked him sarcastically, pointing to it with her quirt. "I'm sure it would taste just as good as those—those—" She retched dryly.

"The Indians don't eat buffalo hearts," he told her. "They leave them here on the prairie after a kill to help regenerate the herds."

War Pony, who had observed Cimarron's action and heard his comments, nodded, a glint in his eyes. "You," he said. "Good buffalo hunter. But not as good as War Pony."

"Nor near as nimble as you neither," Cimarron responded with a grin. "The way you leaped out of the way of that bull—I do declare you'd do credit to a circus performer."

"Take meat," War Pony said.

Cimarron sliced off some of the loin and packed it in grass before putting it in his saddle bag. "I'll turn it into jerky first chance I get."

"We go," War Pony said to him some time later. He

raised his right hand and brushed it upward from his lips, his eyes on Cimarron, who responded by also making the sign for friend.

He watched the Cheyennes ride away leading their heavily laden packhorses and then turned to Beatrice. "Been nice knowing you, honey. Maybe we'll meet again some time. I hope we do, I truly do."

"You're riding west after Farley?"

"I am." He bent down to check the bay's cinch strap.

He was tightening it when he heard Beatrice come up behind him. He started to turn, saw the bloody buffalo skull she held high in both hands.

Beatrice brought her improvised weapon down to crash against the side of Cimarron's head.

He staggered under the blow, heard a roaring in his ears, and then, as blood from the buffalo skull ran down his face, he fell to his knees and a moment later, hit the ground, the roaring suddenly silent as he lay unconscious at Beatrice's feet.

3

The terrible heat of a fire he could feel but not see burned Cimarron's body. The fire grew hotter and he tried to turn away from it but it was everywhere and nowhere and it was consuming him.

Nor could he escape the pain in the muscles of his arms and legs. Pain also wrenched his wrists and ankles.

A black fog blinded him and he tried to fight his way out of it only to find himself sinking deeper and deeper into it.

Laughter suddenly rippled through the fog. He tried to cry out for help to the woman who had laughed but he could utter no sound.

He tried to run but he could not move a muscle.

Gradually, the fog began to dissipate but the pain did not.

He groaned.

The laughter again, mirthless and cold.

He opened his lips to speak but no sound came from them. He tried to open his eyes. One did open and he saw the blazing sun directly above him. His other eye, which was clotted shut by his own blood that had flowed from his scalp wound after Beatrice had struck him, remained closed. He looked away from the sun, turned his head first one way and then the other, and realized that he was lying naked on his back in the midst of the bloody remains of the dead buffaloes.

Beatrice was standing above him and staring down at him, her quirt in one hand, a knife in the other. She no longer laughed.

He tried to rise but found that he could move no part of his body except his head. He turned and saw that his arms were stretched out and tied with wet strips of rawhide to two wooden stakes that were driven deep into the ground. He raised his head and saw that his legs were spread and his ankles were also bound to two stakes by means of wet strips of rawhide. There were, he judged, a good three or four inches of rawhide stretching between his hands and feet and the stakes to which the strips were fastened.

The fire he had felt before regaining consciousness was, he now realized, the sun beating down on him as he lay staked out and helpless beneath it. The pain he felt was the result of the way his body and limbs had been stretched to their limit and also from the rawhide, which was biting into his ankles and wrists. That pain would worsen, he knew, as the rawhide strips began to dry and, as they dried, shrink.

He turned his head and saw his bay standing some distance away. His rifle, he noted, remained in its boot. In the opposite direction lay his clothes, boots, and cartridge belt, his Colt still in its holster. Next to them, Beatrice's horse stood sweating.

He stared at her with his one good eye and licked his lips with the little saliva he had left in his mouth. "Why?" he asked her, his voice a cracked whisper.

"Why?" she repeated, practically screaming the word. She tossed her head and her hair flew about it. "I'll tell you why. Because you were the cause of my brother's death, that's why!"

"Your brother," he repeated numbly.

"My full name," Beatrice said, "is Beatrice Spinks."

Cimarron's body went limp. His eye closed.

"Two years ago it was," she said, her voice low. "You arrested Tillman for murder. You took him to Fort Smith to stand trial. Judge Parker sentenced him to hang. He did hang. *Because of you!*"

The depraved face of Tillman Spinks glowed in the darkness behind Cimarron's eyes. He had seen the man hang on the gallows in the stone-walled compound of Fort Smith. His one eye opened and fastened on Beatrice.

"Since he died—since you *caused* him to die—" she snarled, "I've been after you. There were several times when I almost had you but something or someone always intervened. I told you that I was about to be married. That was true. There was a man who loved me. I left him because I hated you more than I loved him. I set out to find you. To kill you. I talked to people who knew you to learn your habits. Alma

Ralston was just one of those people I met in my travels who knew you.''

"You finally caught up with me.''

"Finally.'' Beatrice breathed the word as if it were a prayer. She stared down at Cimarron with her hate-filled black eyes and continued, "I knew you had seen me back on the trail so I rode north into the woods intending to pick you off the first chance I got.''

"A call of nature, you said.'' He tried a laugh which emerged as a moan from between his parched lips.

"Before I could shoot you, Farley came after you. I couldn't let him kill you. You were—you *are*—mine, Cimarron. I drove Farley off. I tried to kill him but failed. Not that it mattered. What did matter at the time was to get rid of him one way or another and, when I had done that, I joined you.''

"Last night—when you were prowling around—you were looking for your rifle.''

"I was. I intended to wake you, tell you who I was, and then shoot you.''

"Good thing for me I had your rifle tucked away in my bedroll.''

"Then those damned Cheyennes appeared this morning. I tried to keep you away from them but you rode up to them so I still couldn't make my move. Once they had gone and you told me you were heading west after Farley, I knew I had to do something because I had told you I was heading north and there was no way I could travel west with you without you becoming suspicious of my motives.

"At first, I was simply going to shoot you in the back after telling you who I was. But then I had another idea—a much better one.''

"What idea did you have, honey?''

Beatrice lashed out with her quirt.

Its braided leather slashed Cimarron's face and he gritted his teeth against the pain it had caused him.

"Don't you ever call me that again!'' Beatrice screamed at him. "Last night—when we were together last night—I forced myself to make love to you. It was the only way I could hold you. I thought you might ride off when I was asleep. *I am not your 'honey!'* I'm your executioner, Cimarron, the way you were Tillman's executioner.''

"I didn't hang him.''

"He wouldn't have been hanged if it were not for you."

"I suppose you'll be going after Judge Parker and George Maledon once you've done for me. They're both old men and ought to be easier to handle than me. Once you've gotten rid of Tillman's judge and hangman, why, then you can go on back home and marry that man you said you loved and you can set up housekeeping, the two of you."

Beatrice's quirt whistled through the air and landed on Cimarron, cutting into his flesh and forming a thin red line across his bare chest.

Her lips parted in a cruel smile. "When I saw that some meat was left on these buffalo bones, I realized what was going to happen."

Cimarron remained silent, watching her while forcing himself to endure the pain that was racking his body as the rawhide thongs dried, turning slowly from black to tan. He tried to resist their pull on his limbs and body but was unable to do so.

"Vultures and coyotes will come for that meat. For you too, Cimarron."

"Buzzards and coyotes prefer dead meat. I'm still alive though maybe not exactly kicking seeing as how you staked me out so nice and neat while I was unconscious."

"You'll be nearly dead because of what I intend to do to you. But I won't kill you. I want them to eat you alive. As far as the buzzards and coyotes are concerned, they'll probably think you are dead because you won't be able to move. You won't be able to drive them off. I intend to watch the spectacle. I intend to enjoy it immensely. When the scavengers have killed you, I'll go home."

"But not to your daddy's ranch in the Unassigned Lands."

"My father is dead. That was just another lie I told you in order to travel with you. Look, Cimarron!" Beatrice pointed to the sky.

He looked up, his one good eye on the lone turkey buzzard lazily circling in the sky above him and the remains of the slaughtered buffalo. He winced and then cried out in pain a moment later as Beatrice used her knife to make a long shallow cut in the flesh of his left thigh.

He winced again as her knife sliced the flesh of his right thigh. He felt the blood oozing from the wounds and running down his legs. He tried to swallow but couldn't because his mouth was too dry.

"I could use some water," he said, closing his one good eye. "You wouldn't want me to die of thirst, would you? It would spoil your fun if I went and died like that on you."

He felt liquid drip on his lips and he simultaneously opened them and his one eye to discover by taste and by sight that the liquid was his own blood which dripped from the knife Beatrice was holding above his lips. He swallowed the blood in silence, knowing that she would give him no water.

He lay motionless, watching the four buzzards that now circled in the sky above him. How long would it take, he wondered, for the coyotes to come. Not long, he decided. They wouldn't have to wait until they scented buffalo flesh stinking beneath the sun. They already had a signal that would alert them to the presence of carrion on the plain. Four signals, in fact—the four buzzards that now wheeled in the sky.

He stared steadily at the dripping knife in Beatrice's hand. Soon, it no longer dripped.

It descended.

Cimarron swore to himself that he would not cry out this time no matter how severe the pain. But, as Beatrice drew the blade of her knife from the base of his throat and down along his chest to his navel, he broke his oath. His wordless cry erupted until he silenced it by clenching his teeth together, causing the muscles in his jaws to twitch. He felt . . .

No!

She wouldn't—

He looked down the length of his body and saw his limp flesh resting on the bloody blade of the knife Beatrice still held in her hand as she knelt on the ground beside him.

Her lips parted in a chilling smile. "What would Alma Ralston say if she knew you'd lost this?" She moved the knife slightly so that he appeared to have become erect.

Cimarron strained at the thongs binding him, wanting to kick out at her, wanting to strike her. He wanted, he realized, to kill her. He could feel his hands circling her slender throat. He felt exultation arise within him as his grip tightened and she gagged and tore desperately at his unyielding fingers. . . .

Beatrice stood up.

Cimarron braced himself, wondering what her next move would be.

An unseen coyote yipped in the distance.

"It won't be long now," she said, excitement sharpening her tone. "The coyotes are coming."

"I prefer their company to yours, honey."

Down came the quirt to slash again into the flesh of Cimarron's face, sending his head jerking wildly to one side.

Blood ran into his mouth. He swallowed it.

Beatrice, leading her horse, began to walk away from him.

"You're leaving? This party of yours is just getting going."

"I'm not leaving," she said without turning back to him. "I'm going to sit in the shade of those trees over there and I'm going to watch you die."

"I've met a whole lot of women in my time," he called out to her. "But never one that took her pleasure in the twisted fashion you do."

Beatrice walked on without responding to his taunt.

With a whir of heavy wings, a buzzard landed near Cimarron.

He watched it compose its wings, arch its long neck, and blink the beady eyes set in its bald head.

The bird's head suddenly shot out and down and its beak tore into a ragged piece of flesh that was clinging to a buffalo bone. When it had devoured the meat, it arched its neck again and stared at Cimarron.

The other three buzzards came down then in a flurry of wings and began to hop about in the carrion, pecking at it and at each other as they fought for their share of the meat.

Cimarron concentrated on the thongs that bound him, trying to ignore the buzzards and the threat they represented to him. His foot touched something. He raised his head and looked down along the length of his body. His left foot was touching the stake to which it was bound, having been inexorably drawn toward it as the rawhide dried in the hot sun.

He pressed the sole of his foot against the stake and, as he did so, pain shot up his leg and into his pelvis. His leg seemed about to tear itself free of its socket. With sweat sliding down his forehead and face and pain possessing his limbs and the rest of his body, he continued to press his foot against the stake. He felt it move slightly and he almost forgot the pain shrieking within him.

He angled his foot to the left and managed to hook his

44

instep around the stake. He pulled his foot toward him. The stake moved again as another buzzard landed near him.

As he continued trying to pull the stake from the ground, sweat ran into his one good eye, blinding it. But he did not need that eye to see what he was doing. He continued pulling on and then alternately pushing against the stake. He braced his heel against it and shoved. Exultation seized him as he felt the stake give way and then pull out of the ground. Quickly, he turned his head and, blinking the stinging sweat out of his eye, he searched for Beatrice. He spotted her in the distance, a shadowy figure seated at the edge of the trees the buffalo herd had rounded earlier. She was, he hoped, too far away from him to be able to see what he had just done.

He went to work on the stake that bound his other leg and ducked his head as another buzzard landed on the ground and dust flew up from beneath it.

The buzzard, its wings still flapping, hopped up to him and its beak began to tear at his bloody chest.

"Git!" he shouted, resisting the impulse to hit out at the ugly bird with his left leg in order not to betray to Beatrice the fact that part of him was now free.

The vulture eyed him without moving. Another one, its wings partly spread as if ready for flight, joined the first.

My eyes, Cimarron thought. They'll go for my eyes. Once I'm blinded, they'll have a better chance to get me. He turned his head away from the two buzzards and continued trying to pull the second stake from the ground, his arms and torso stretched to their limits as he fought to give his foot enough room to maneuver the stake.

When he finally succeeded in pulling the stake from the ground, he wanted to shout in triumph but he didn't. Instead, he eased his body upward along the ground, moving slowly in order not to reveal to Beatrice what he was doing, and gripped with both hands the stakes to which his wrists were bound.

But before he could pull them free, a coyote appeared and darted in among the feeding buzzards. Its sharp teeth closed on Cimarron's right forearm.

He ripped both stakes from the ground and swung his fists at the coyote.

It went bounding off into the distance and the startled buzzards flapped away from him.

He staggered to his feet and then made a dash toward his horse.

He fell before he reached it and the breath was knocked from his lungs. He pulled himself up onto his hands and knees and then, when he had managed to stand, he ran shakily toward the bay.

A rifle shot went whistling past him.

He reached his horse before Beatrice could fire again, positioned himself behind it, and pulled his Winchester from its boot. Leaning against the bay for support, he took quick aim and fired at Beatrice, aiming high with the intention of driving her off.

The coyote let out a yip and went racing away to disappear among the trees. The vultures rose into the air and then settled down upon the ground again to resume their feeding.

Beatrice returned his fire and her shot grazed the bay's neck.

As the horse bolted, Cimarron was knocked to one side. He fell to the ground, dropping his rifle as he did so. His head hit a rock and the sun suddenly dimmed. He tried to rise, his vision blurring, his right hand groping blindly for his rifle. With his left hand, he clawed at his eye which was still closed because of the clotted blood covering it.

When he could see again with both eyes, he found his rifle and sprang to his feet. He stood there, swaying and blinking in the bright glare of the sun.

She was coming toward him now and riding hard. He fired, aiming to one side of her but his warning shot didn't stop her.

She raised her rifle as she rode toward Cimarron whose vision suddenly blurred again and he wondered how to stop her without having to wound—or worse—kill her.

His hesitation was a mistake.

Beatrice got off another shot and this time she hit Cimarron in the right shoulder.

His body involuntarily spun around as his fingers opened and his Winchester fell from his hands. Reflexively, his left hand reached for the wound on his right shoulder. His foot struck a stone and he teetered a moment, both arms flailing wildly, and then fell face down in the warm grass.

Gasping, his chest heaving, he rolled over and saw Beatrice looming ever larger in the distance as she continued riding toward him. He reached out and his right hand closed on his rifle, a red rage seething within him. He raised it, took aim as Beatrice was about to squeeze off another shot, and fired.

She made no sound as the bullet slammed into her chest. She dropped the reins, seeming to lean backward in the saddle, and then she fell from it, her horse running on toward Cimarron without her.

He took a deep breath and, unmindful of the wounds she had inflicted upon him with her knife and rifle, rose to his feet, staring at her body lying in the grass not far from him.

The rage he had felt when he had fired at her began to cool and be replaced by a sense of awe at what he had done. Had he intended to shoot her? The answer was clear. He had. She would have killed him if he hadn't fought back. He was certain of that fact. But he had never killed a woman before.

He took a step toward Beatrice. Maybe he hadn't killed her. He hoped he hadn't but he was almost sure . . . He took another step. And then a third.

When he reached her, she did not move. Her eyes stared—sightlessly, he realized—up at the sun that stared back unperturbed. He got down on one knee and pressed two fingers against her neck. No pulse, not the faintest. His head dropped down and he propped it up with one hand, his elbow braced on his knee.

Nausea flooded him.

He swallowed several times and at last the nausea subsided.

I have to bury her, he told himself. I've got no shovel, he reminded himself. He looked off into the distance at the vultures, which were still feeding. The coyote, he noticed, was back. It wasn't alone. It and three companions warily circled the carnage, occasionally darting forward to seize a bone and then quickly withdraw as the vultures chased them away.

They'll get her, he thought, and the nausea returned.

He got to his feet, conscious of the stakes that were dangling from their rawhide thongs, which were still attached to his wrists and ankles. He looked down at Beatrice.

She had intended to kill him. She had tried hard to do so. He had defended himself. It was that simple. He thought of her brother, Tillman Spinks, and knew that it was also that complicated.

She had intended that the buzzards and the coyotes should have him. But the world had turned and fate had decreed that they would have her instead.

He grimaced and staggered away from her body. Keeping his eyes on the bay, which had stopped in the distance, he made his way toward the horse. On the way, he picked up his clothes and cartridge belt. Carrying them and his rifle, he moved unsteadily across the plain as the sun burned his body and pain wracked it.

When he finally reached his horse, a journey that seemed to him to have taken him hours to complete, he sat down on the ground in the shade of the bay's shadow. He sat there for several minutes without moving and then he slowly began to dress after removing the stakes from his wrists and ankles.

I'm in trouble, he told himself, as he pulled on his boots, using only his left hand because his right arm was weak and trembling, the result of Beatrice's bullet in his shoulder. He fastened his cartridge belt around his hips.

I need help, he thought. But who's going to give it to me way the hell out here on the plain? He didn't like the answer that came to him. No one. Because there was no one out here except himself. No one alive. He avoided looking at Beatrice.

He suddenly realized that he had been wrong. True, there was no one nearby. But there was help available. Could he get to where that help was?

He didn't know. He did know that he had no other choice but to try or die from one or more of several possible causes among which were loss of blood and infection.

He rose and examined his bay's neck. Blood streaked it but the animal's flesh wound was not serious. He booted his rifle and then placed his left foot in the stirrup. He swung clumsily into the saddle, the effort of doing so sending pain shooting down his right arm, picked up the reins, and walked the horse west.

The trail that stretched out before him became a path of pain. The day through which he rode along it became an arena of agony.

The blood from his bullet and knife wounds dried, welding patches of his clothing to his body which sometimes, when he moved a certain way, tore free of the wounds, opening them again. He gripped the horn of his saddle with both hands as he rode along, weariness constantly threatening to overwhelm him, determined to stay in the saddle until he reached his destination.

But his determination faltered as the sun set and, when he suddenly awoke from a deep sleep and found himself sliding out of the saddle, he surrendered to the exhaustion that was as much a part of him now as were his blood and bones.

He got out of the saddle and, without bothering to care for his horse or to open his bedroll, he lay down on the ground, tied the bay's reins around his right wrist, and fell asleep instantly. He awoke an unmeasured amount of time later to find the sun in the sky and a thirst raging within him. Groggily, he sat up, removed his canteen that was hanging from his saddle horn, drank from it, and fell asleep again as he was stoppering it.

He awoke once during the night and lay on his back staring up at the stars. They vanished as he slept once more. It was mid-morning when he awoke again, no longer exhausted but not refreshed.

He was hot, sweating in fact. But he was lying in the shade that was being cast by a lone loblolly pine. He ran a hand along the stubble covering his cheeks and chin. His skin felt hot to his touch. The aching of his body seemed to have intensified during the time he had slept.

Fever, he thought.

Those cuts she made in me are full of dirt from the times I fell before I got my clothes back on. Add to that the fact that my clothes themselves are none too clean . . .

How far did he have to ride? There was no way to be sure. He guessed he might reach his destination by sundown if he set out now.

He climbed aboard the bay and moved out, his lips set in a grim line, his eyes watering, and the sweat running in thin rivulets down his face and body.

The sound of the bay's harness jingling intensified until it sounded to him like a brass band gone berserk. A roadrunner that crossed his path, its long tail feathers twitching, suddenly became three roadrunners. He blinked. There was only one roadrunner now. I'm seeing things, he thought. Damned fever's to blame.

As the sun slipped low in the sky, despair rose within him. The place for which he was headed was too big. He'd never find anyone on it. Five million acres! No, less than that because three years ago the government had sheared off some seven hundred and sixty thousand acres, which it had handed over to the Wichitas and the Affiliated Bands. But that still left a lot of land to hunt around in even if a man was up to hunting. He knew he wasn't. But what else am I to do, he asked himself and rode relentlessly on.

He saw her in the distance—or thought he saw her.

Small, dark. Gathering firewood. As he spurred his horse and rode toward her, she saw him. She stood rigid for a moment and then dropped the wood she had gathered from a deadfall and turned away. She ran.

He tried to cry out to her but no sound came from between his lips. He waved but her back was to him.

He waved again and fell forward, hitting his horse's neck. He clutched the bay's mane in both hands to steady himself and then straightened up.

"Ho!"

As the word was torn from his throat so was the air from his lungs. He felt himself slipping and clutched desperately at his horse's mane. The animal protested by shaking its head. He lost his grip on the bay's mane and slid out of the saddle.

He hit the ground with a thud and the bay stood staring down at him. His eyes closed. His fingers clawed at the grass.

Darkness came to him.

Then, light again.

He opened his eyes and then turned his head at the sound of a soft footfall. She was still there, staring at him from the distance, her eyes narrowed, her hands stiff at her sides.

"Help me," he said and wondered if she had heard him and suspecting that, if she had, she would not understand the words he had spoken because she was an Indian and might never have learned English.

But wasn't there a school . . . He couldn't complete the thought and when he looked for her again she was gone.

He summoned every ounce of energy that remained to him by sheer force of will and got up from the ground. He reached out for the bay but it stepped away from him. He spoke softly to it and was able to get one hand on his saddle horn and one boot in the stirrup. Up, he commanded himself. Do it. Now!

He never made it back into the saddle. His right leg swung

up and struck the rump of the horse. He lost his hold on the saddle horn and fell to the ground again.

Carrie, who had no last name, was suddenly lying beside him, and he tried to reach out to touch her but he couldn't lift his hand. She whispered something he didn't catch to him and then she put a finger on his lips and told him not to talk. There were better things to do, she assured him. But he couldn't do them and he tried to explain why to her but Carrie, pouting, rose and vanished.

He was alone then, neither asleep nor awake but decidedly feverish.

The light was fading. Or was it that he couldn't see very well?

A man stood watching him and he shuddered when he recognized the figure. He tried to turn away but the man barked a command and he continued to meet the dead man's gaze and listen as the man condemned him for what he had done.

"—Mistake," he muttered.

"Murder!" thundered the man.

He winced and grew suddenly icy.

"Cold-blooded murder!" roared the man with the dead and empty eyes.

He said, "Pa, I—"

But his father had disappeared, leaving behind him only his indictment, which still chilled Cimarron as he lay on the ground unable to move or to think clearly.

He began to smile then as scores of hallucinatory roadrunners began to circle him, talking among themselves of insects and eggs and the mating season. He told them he understood their point of view and, gratified, they buried him beneath a pile of soft feathers, which blinded him.

Someone was singing at the far edge of his darkening world.

Who? He looked around but saw no one. Not at first. And then she was there. He couldn't remember her name. But he remembered how lovely she had been. He called out to her, not with words but with desire and she came to him again as she had done all those other times and her kiss was sweet and her hands were gentle. He wanted to weep with relief, but he didn't. He let her hold him close to her and he knew he was safe again at last in the arms of a woman who would hold back the bullets and shunt aside the knives so that he would live and together they would . . .

"Dead."

"Sick."

He opened his eyes and saw the two men who had just spoken. The girl he had seen earlier was with them. The two Indians were standing beside him and looking down at him.

"Wa—" he said.

The two men looked at each other and then one of them turned to him and asked, "You want water?"

"Wa—" he said again. The words wouldn't come. He had to *make* them come. He finally succeeded in forcing them from between his lips. "War Pony."

"You know him?" one of the men asked.

Cimarron, his eyes closed, repeated, "War Pony." And then he plunged down into a darkness that was riotous with redly blazing bursts of jagged light.

4

Inferno.

The word was a repetitive murmur in Cimarron's mind.

The sun must be beating down upon me, he thought, because my body's hot and wet all over with sweat. His left hand stirred. It touched his leg. I'm naked again, he thought with vague surprise.

Hissssss.

Snake, he thought. Got to move fast. The snake—where?

He opened his eyes wide and stared wildly about him but he could see nothing except the clouds of smoke—no, he corrected himself—steam.

Hissssss.

The roiling clouds of steam billowed up around and above him.

Through a gap in them, Cimarron saw an arched dome above him and he realized where he was and what the meaning of the hissing sound he had heard was. He peered through the steam and was finally able to make out the shadowy figure of a man standing in the middle of the sweat lodge.

War Pony was pouring water from a bark vessel over heated stones that lay piled on the ground beneath the arching frame of the sweat lodge, which was made of bent saplings lashed together with rawhide and covered with buffalo robes.

The steam closed around War Pony, hiding him from sight.

Cimarron's fingers stirred and he felt the buffalo robe beneath him. He lay still, letting himself become aware of every part of his body. His thighs throbbed from the cuts Beatrice had inflicted on them. His shoulder sent stark messages of pain to his brain, but his arms and legs no longer ached the way they had, nor was his head aching now.

War Pony materialized beside him.

"I had no place else to go," Cimarron told him apologetically.

War Pony nodded. "Your fire burns low now?"

"It does. The fever's about broke, feels like."

"Good. Doctor comes to take out bullet."

"Medicine man?"

"White doctor at Darlington Agency."

"There's a doctor there now?"

"Since time of planting moon."

"I met a girl," Cimarron began.

"Antelope," War Pony said. "She went for help after she feared you no more."

"There were two men with her."

"They brought you here because you spoke my name."

"I'm sorry to go and cause you all this trouble, War Pony. I needed help—"

War Pony interrupted Cimarron by saying, "I am glad to give it. I remember what happened on the hunt. An Elk Soldier pays his debts."

"I'll be out from under your feet real quick. Maybe today." A thought occurred to Cimarron. "How long've I been on the reservation?"

War Pony held up three fingers.

"Three days, huh?"

Dim sunlight flowed into the sweat lodge as the buffalo robe at its entrance was suddenly raised.

War Pony stepped to one side and Cimarron saw the white man whose gaunt face wore an expression of concern come into the lodge and walk up to him, a black leather satchel in his hand. The man's hair was thinning and graying but his mustache, which hid his upper lip, was still brown and his black eyes were sharp.

"Doc, I'm glad to see you."

"How are you feeling?"

"I'm feeling a whole lot better than I was a while back, I can tell you, thanks to War Pony."

The doctor knelt on the ground and placed the back of his hand against Cimarron's forehead. "I was told you had a fever but it looks like this sweat lodge has done its work well." He quickly scanned Cimarron's body. "War Pony, I could use some water—hot water."

War Pony, a moment later, handed the doctor his bark vessel, which he had filled with hot water.

"I'm Cassius Tolliver," the doctor told Cimarron as he went to work on his patient's legs and chest.

"I'm called Cimarron, Doc."

Cimarron winced as Tolliver opened his wounds and let the blood flow for a moment before washing them, applying a thick brown salve, and then bandaging them.

"That'll do for your legs and chest," Tolliver said when he had finished. "Now let's have a look at your shoulder." He carefully examined the bullet wound and then opened his satchel.

"What's in that bottle, Doc?" Cimarron asked.

"Chloroform in solution. I'm going to soak a cloth with it and you're going to breathe it in. Once you are anesthetized, I'll dig that bullet out of you."

Cimarron shook his head. "I don't want any of that stuff, Doc. I saw a man die of a heart attack after a doctor fed him that stuff."

"Cardiac paralysis induced by the administration of chloroform is a statistically rare event," Tolliver declared somewhat testily. "It may occur once in, oh, several thousand cases."

"I don't want to be that one rare case where it happens, Doc."

"Chloroform is far superior to ether in that it is not flammable and . . ."

"Doc, I'd be obliged to you if you'd just get your knife and get to work on that bullet that's buried somewhere in my shoulder. I'll try hard to grin and bear what you've got to do."

Tolliver hesitated a moment and then shrugged. He opened his satchel, rummaged about in it, and removed a thin blade that had a curved point and a bone handle. "You're sure you want it this way?" he asked hesitantly.

"Get on with it, Doc."

Tolliver bent down, and Cimarron, as the sharp blade probed his wound, clenched his fists and gritted his teeth. His body went rigid. He felt his fingernails digging into the palms of his hands and he heard his teeth grinding together.

"I've got to open you up a bit more," Tolliver told him.

As the probing continued, Cimarron let out a moan.

War Pony was suddenly beside him. "Take this." He offered Cimarron an arrowhead.

Cimarron understood at once. He took the flint arrowhead, placed it between his teeth, and bit down hard on it.

Tolliver went on working in silence. "Found it," he muttered some moments later.

Cimarron's pain lessened but then Tolliver took another instrument from his satchel and, as he inserted it into the wound, the pain increased. Cimarron bit down on the arrowhead between his teeth.

"Got it," Tolliver exclaimed a moment later.

Cimarron relaxed and took the arrowhead from between his teeth as Tolliver proceeded to wash his shoulder wound and then, after applying salve to it, bandage it.

As the doctor stood up, Cimarron said, "I'll pay you for your trouble once I find my jeans, Doc."

"There will be no need for that," Tolliver said as he repacked his satchel. "The government pays me a stipend for the work I do here on the reservation which is, if not munificent, at least generous." He smiled wryly. "Adequate, I suppose, would be the precise word."

"I'm much obliged to you, Doc."

"War Pony," Tolliver said, "I think you can take him out of here now. Is there room in someone's lodge for him until he's healed?"

"He will live in the lodge of Big Eagle," War Pony replied. "I go now to bring help to take him there."

"Whew!" Tolliver exclaimed when War Pony had gone. "This place is like something Dante might have imagined."

"Funny you should mention that, Doc. When I woke up in here I was thinking much the same thing. Inferno, is what I was thinking. That made me think of Dante when he was just about to enter hell which is where I thought for a minute I might be. Anyway, he keeps hearing the lost souls lamenting and he asks Virgil what they're making such a fuss about and Virgil, if I remember right, says, 'I will tell you very briefly. These have no hope of death; existence here is so degraded and obscure, that they are envious of any other lot.' Well, Doc, that about sums up how I felt when I woke up in here."

Tolliver studied Cimarron a moment. "I don't usually ask personal questions of my patients. But you intrigue me—

especially so when I hear you quoting Dante. The Second Canto, wasn't it?''

"Third."

"How did you happen to come here, Cimarron?"

Cimarron told him.

"So you're a lawman," Tolliver mused. "A lawman who reads Dante."

"Him and other writers. Did you ever happen to see Gustave Doré's illustrations for *The Divine Comedy*, Doc?"

"I have, yes. Impressive."

"Impressive? Why, Doc, every time I looked at one of the ones he did for the Inferno, it sent shivers clear through me. If that's what hell's like, I'd best be about mending my sinful ways real soon."

Tolliver smiled. "I want you to rest and—"

Cimarron managed to sit up. "I've got to be riding out of here, Doc. Today maybe. I've got to catch that horse thief I mentioned to you before."

"Leave the man to his thieving for now. You're in no condition to travel. Granted that you're young and the young heal quickly, I still insist that you remain with Big Eagle until I say you are well enough to leave the reservation."

Cimarron let it go, deciding not to argue the point.

Moments after the doctor had left the sweat lodge, War Pony reappeared within it, Nine Fingers at his side.

The steam was almost all gone now because the stones had cooled and Cimarron could see the two men clearly. War Pony was the more impressive of the pair if a muscular frame was important, he thought. But Nine Fingers, stolidly built with a hooked nose and eyes that bored into a man, was obviously no weakling. Both men clearly possessed strength. But War Pony, Cimarron noticed, was not only strong but also graceful in his movements, reminding Cimarron of a cougar.

Without a word, both men bent down and helped him to his feet. They waited while he wrapped the buffalo robe he had been lying on around his naked body and then, placing his arms over their shoulders, they left the sweat lodge.

Antelope stood outside it and Cimarron smiled at her and said, "I'm obliged to you for getting me some help."

Her black eyes stared into Cimarron's but she said nothing.

"I guess she doesn't understand English," he remarked to War Pony.

Nine Fingers said, "Antelope understands your tongue. She learns it at the reservation school."

Cimarron, as they left Antelope behind them, glanced over his shoulder and saw her raise a flute to her lips. The flute, he noticed, was made of two grooved halves of a cedar stick that were glued together. It had five finger holes and an air vent.

As the three men continued walking toward Big Eagle's lodge, the thin music of Antelope's flute followed them.

Whirlwind said something to War Pony in the Cheyenne language and War Pony laughed heartily.

"You going to let me in on the joke?" Cimarron asked and then grunted in pain as he stumbled over a stone.

"Antelope," War Pony said, "makes music with medicine flute to catch you."

"To catch me?" Cimarron blurted out in surprise. "Why, she's nothing more'n a baby."

"Soon she will be a woman," Nine Fingers said matter-of-factly.

"You are already a man," War Pony stated as matter-of-factly.

"But she don't hardly even know me!" Cimarron protested.

"What must she know about you to want you?" War Pony asked.

Cimarron shook his head in dismay and was still shaking it when the flute music had faded away and they were standing in front of the lodge of Big Eagle.

Cimarron, noting that its flap was closed, said, "I guess we better let out a yell or something to let Big Eagle know we're out here if he's in there."

War Pony and Nine Fingers exchanged glances.

Cimarron, noting the mute exchange between the two men, said, "I'm not altogether ignorant of the ways of the Plains Indians. I wouldn't go barging in on a man unless his lodge flap was already open."

War Pony called out something in Cheyenne and was answered in the same language by a male voice that came from inside the lodge.

Nine Fingers drew back the flap and they entered the lodge, all of them moving to the right.

58

At the rear of the lodge, seated cross legged, was an old man with white hair worn in unadorned braids. His eyes were on Cimarron's face and they did not blink. His seamed face was expressionless and Cimarron began to feel uneasy.

The old man spoke.

War Pony translated the words. "My father says you are welcome in his lodge. He says he hopes you will be well soon. He says you are to sit in the guest place."

"I'll try making it on my own now." Cimarron withdrew his arms from the shoulders of War Pony and Nine Fingers. He walked around the fire that burned in the center of the lodge and gingerly seated himself to the left of Big Eagle.

"War Pony, you tell Big Eagle for me I'm grateful for his hospitality."

War Pony did and then, after a murmured conversation with Nine Fingers, he sat down facing Cimarron as Nine Fingers left the lodge.

Big Eagle coughed, a dry sound in the stillness. He bent forward, his hands pressed against his thin chest.

"Much sickness here," War Pony said. "In the North, we live and be well. Here, our people get sick. Many have died. Some are sick now like Big Eagle. Many more will die if we cannot go north."

"You want to go back to the Red Cloud Agency, is that it?"

War Pony nodded. "Some of our people say they will go. Agent Tracy say they will not."

Big Eagle spoke in guttural tones.

"My father," War Pony said, "heard you. He understands some white words. He says we must go back to the Dakota Hills."

"But the Dakotas are crawling with prospectors. They're no place for the Cheyennes now."

A sardonic smile appeared on War Pony's face. "Do you know of a place for the Cheyennes now?"

Big Eagle spoke rapidly.

"My father may be right," War Pony said, his smile gone. "He says we will make a place for our people."

"You go and jump the reservation," Cimarron said slowly, "and you'll have the cavalry coming after you faster'n sun can melt snow."

"We have fought the cavalry before," War Pony said with no show of emotion. "We can do the same again."

"And maybe die in the doing. Here you've got food, your annuities—"

Big Eagle spat into the fire and grunted several consonantal words in Cheyenne.

War Pony translated, "Annuities come late. But no corn. No flour. Provisions not last. Beef for the people is sickly and not enough. Buffalo almost all gone. Sometimes we are not permitted to hunt."

Big Eagle made several signs in quick succession, his eyes on Cimarron.

Cimarron understood. "I know it's hard to watch your women and children go hungry. But it'll be real hard on them if they have to watch their warriors die from soldiers' bullets."

"A man does well to die fighting when he cannot get food for his women and children," War Pony said and then suddenly lapsed into the Cheyenne language.

"I don't know how to talk your language," Cimarron told him.

The Cheyenne, upon realizing that he had been speaking in his own language, said, "I said there are times when an Elk Soldier must fight the ones who hurt his people. I said, if he dies fighting, it would be good for him to let his soul go from his body to travel on the Hanging Road toward the Wise One Above, to Heammawihio."

"The Hanging Road," Cimarron repeated. "What's that?"

"You call it the Milky Way."

Cimarron started to say something but, before he could do so, a female voice called from outside the lodge.

War Pony answered in Cheyenne and the lodge flap was raised. Antelope entered and stepped shyly to the left.

Big Eagle nodded and she walked around the fire to stop in front of Cimarron.

One hand came out from under her blanket and she held it out to him.

He took the necklace of bear's claws from her and said, "Thank you, Antelope."

"Bear heals his own wounds," she said. She pointed to the necklace and then to Cimarron's neck. "Bear claws strong medicine for a man who is hurt."

Cimarron put the necklace on.

Antelope quickly turned and as quickly left the lodge.

"You sleep now," War Pony told Cimarron. "We go to talk to other Elk Soldiers."

War Pony left the lodge and, a moment later, so did Big Eagle.

Cimarron moved toward the wall of the lodge, wrapped the buffalo robe around him, and lay down on the ground. As he closed his eyes, he heard the echoes of War Pony's words, which he had found disturbing. As he shifted position, the bear claws around his neck clicked. He reached up and touched them, smiling and thinking of Antelope.

A number of days after his arrival on the reservation, Cimarron stood outside the pole corral with an excited group of Cheyenne women and children watching War Pony, Nine Fingers, and other braves slaughter the cattle that were milling about among the men inside the corral.

He grimaced as Nine Fingers swung a pole axe that landed on the skull of a steer but did not kill the animal. As the steer went bellowing away from Nine Fingers, its brain bulging from its broken skull, Nine Fingers pursued it and delivered a second blow that felled the animal but did not stop its terrified bellowing.

Gouts of blood flew through the air as the Cheyenne men continued to axe and lance the cattle. The bellowing of the animals thundered on as the slaughter continued and dust rose to fill the air.

"You're the man they call Cimarron."

Cimarron turned and saw a thin, dour man of middle age and average height standing behind him. The man's eyes were a pale blue, almost blending with the whites surrounding them. His sunken cheeks were clean-shaven, as was his chin, and his ears jutted out from the sides of his head.

"I hope you're recuperating," the man said and held out his hand. "I'm Enoch Tracy, the Indian agent for this reservation."

Cimarron shook Tracy's hand and then jerked a thumb over his shoulder. "How come you don't give those men guns to kill their beeves?"

"When the Indians arrive here on the reservation," Tracy said in his slightly rasping voice, "the first thing we do is disarm and then dismount them."

"That so? I can't think of a better way than that to unman a Cheyenne warrior."

Tracy frowned. "Surely you realize it is a necessary procedure? Were the Indians allowed to keep their guns there could be trouble. If they were allowed to keep their ponies, they would very probably, many of them, soon flee the reservation."

"Where'd those beeves come from?" Cimarron asked, turning back toward the corral.

Tracy, after taking a position next to him, answered, "Langley's ranch. He runs cattle up north and I've been able to prevail upon him to sell us some upon occasion."

"Some of them are lame," Cimarron observed. "Most all of them are lean."

"I grant you that they are not the best specimens in the world but they're what Langley agreed to sell us."

Cimarron continued watching War Pony and the other men, all of them bloodied, as they killed the last of the emaciated cattle.

Tracy said, "I have my hands full getting enough beef to feed these people, I can tell you. Many of the ranchers refuse to sell to us because the government cannot compete with the prices the ranchers can get for their stock at the railheads in Kansas. But I do the best I can."

As the butchering of the cattle began, Cimarron said, "Big Eagle said there was no corn or flour handed out with the annuities last time around."

"That's true enough."

"How come you didn't substitute something else?"

"Because we had nothing else. The Indians were, however, given their allotments of dried fruit, rice, beans, coffee, and salt."

"You figure you're feeding these people enough to do more than keep their skin covering their bones?"

Tracy sighed. "I understand your concern, Cimarron, and I must say I share it. But you must understand that my actions are very rigidly proscribed by the commissioner of Indian affairs. I wish I could do more."

"You did, I heard from War Pony, less though."

"I beg your pardon, sir?"

"Each family was to get three pounds of beef." Cimarron glanced at the white men and the scale they were using to weigh the raw beef the Cheyennes were bringing to them. "You cut the ration down to two pounds last week."

"I explained why to them at the time, but they still, many of them, refuse to send their children to our school."

"If I wanted to catch me a rabbit, I wouldn't bait my trap with something bitter."

Tracy studied Cimarron briefly and then said, "I see what you're getting at. But coercion is often the only way to bring civilization's benefits to these people. Many steadfastly refuse to send their children to our school. They can't read or write. The girls cannot sew nor can the boys farm. If we are not allowed to educate them, these children will remain forever wards of the government.

"Already we have children here—very young children and not a few infants—who must be wholly supported by the government because their fathers—and sometimes their mothers too—will not admit their relationships to the infants and children. The Cheyenne society is breaking down. Education in our school is one way we can hope to remedy this unfortunate situation. The older generation may already be lost. I want to save the younger generation."

"You can't save them by starving them."

"What would you suggest I do, given the fact that I am trying my level best to do what is right for these people and given the further fact that I am a civil servant who must obey certain rules and regulations I neither made nor necessarily endorse?"

"Since you asked me for a suggestion, I'll give you one. What I'd do were I you, and the good Lord knows I'm glad I'm not you, is I'd figure out exactly whose side I'm on and if it turned out I found myself on the side of the Cheyennes, why, I'd rear up on my hind legs and fight back against the men who made the regulations that are turning these Cheyennes into beggars with no self-respect and just as much chance for survival as a people."

"I *do* fight for them! Do you want to know what the results of my efforts have been? I'll tell you. I've been accused of insubordination. I've had my appropriations cut. There are those who say I am a poor administrator—wasteful and worse."

"Tracy, I take back what I just said. I ought to learn to mind my own business. You're probably doing the best you can and if I don't happen to think you're going about everything in just the right way, well, I could be wrong. I'm a lawman, not an Indian agent.''

"Cimarron, you remind me of why I came to see you. When I heard that you were here and that you were a United States marshal—''

"Deputy marshal.''

"Yes. Well, I wanted to enlist your aid. We have been severely troubled by whiskey peddlers and horse thieves here on the reservation. No marshal—deputy marshal—has ever been seen this far west before as far as I know so I decided I would ask you if you could help us by trying to apprehend the whiskey peddlers and the horse thieves.''

"I've got no jurisdiction on the reservation.''

"I think we needn't trouble ourselves with the niceties of jurisdictional boundaries. In the past, I've asked the Bureau to assign federal marshals here to help our Indian police keep order on the reservation. My requests have always been refused. Now you're here and you are a federal marshal—''

"But one who's an officer of the court at Fort Smith and Judge Parker's got no say about what goes on here on the reservation.''

"I'd hoped—well, never mind.''

Cimarron caught sight of Antelope in the crowd around the corral. As she watched the weighing of the beef, she licked her lips.

He made up his mind. "I'm hunting a horse thief named Jake Farley. I'll be moseying around out here until I can catch him. Maybe in the meantime I can find time to lend you a hand with your problems.''

"I'd appreciate it, I truly would!'' Tracy exclaimed enthusiastically. "Thank you, Cimarron!''

"Hold on there. I'm not making you any kind of promises. I'm just saying I'll do what I can.''

For War Pony and Big Eagle, he thought. For Antelope. For these men who were once warriors and for these women and children who are being given handouts while their way of life is being destroyed.

"Men have been raiding the Indian pony herds and making off with some of the mounts,'' Tracy said, oblivious of Cimarron's pensiveness. "They strike at random and so far we have been unsuccessful in apprehending them. I know you'll do the job for us.''

"Maybe I will and maybe I won't."

"You mean you won't try? I thought you said—"

"Oh, I'll try all right. What I said ought to tell you something about me."

"Tell me what?"

"That I'm a realistic man, not one who can work anything halfway approaching miracles."

Tracy started to say something but was interrupted by the shout of a man who came running toward the corral, his arms waving, a smile on his face.

He called out in Cheyenne, a stream of words pouring from his lips.

"Trouble?" Cimarron asked Tracy.

"No. That man is Walks with Wolves. He has just announced to the camp that his daughter, Antelope, has now become a woman."

Cimarron glanced in the direction in which he had last seen Antelope, but she had vanished. He gave Tracy a puzzled frown.

Seeing it, the agent said, "Antelope has had her first—uh, passing of blood. It is the custom among the Cheyennes to observe the passage of a girl into womanhood in a rather formal fashion after her father has made his announcement of the fact. Come along and you shall see."

Cimarron accompanied Tracy and most of the Cheyennes back to where the lodges were pitched in a huge circle.

In the center of the circle a huge fire burned.

He watched as the older women ducked under the flap of a lodge in the distance. Some time later, Antelope, followed by the older women, came out of the lodge. She was wearing only a buffalo robe. What he could see of her body was painted a bright red. Her hair was unbraided now and hung down her back, almost reaching her waist. She walked with stately dignity, her head held high, toward the fire.

"The women unbraid the girl's hair," Tracy commented, "and then they paint her entire body red after she has been bathed."

Antelope stopped in front of the fire.

An old woman nudged a burning coal from the fire onto a flat stone and, holding it up on the stone, sprinkled it with juniper needles and white sage, which caused smoke to rise from it.

Antelope bent down over the coal, surrounding it with her robe so that the smoke passed over her entire body. Then, rising, she allowed herself to be led away by the older women.

"She is going to the special lodge where she will remain until her period ends," Tracy explained.

Antelope, as she passed near the spot where Cimarron was standing, turned her head and, when she saw him, her eyes brightened.

Cimarron nodded to her and then turned in the opposite direction as the sound of galloping horses reached his ears.

Warrior Woman was riding into the circle of lodges, leading a string of five ponies. She rode directly to Walks with Wolves and handed him the lead rope, which he willingly took from her.

"I say, this is something of a surprise," Tracy remarked.

"What is?"

"Warrior Woman is proposing that she and Antelope be married. It's rather soon, since the girl has only just become a woman."

"It's rather strange, if you ask me," Cimarron muttered.

"Warrior Woman rides with the men when we allow them to hunt. She considers herself as good, if not better, than any man and considers it degrading to do the work of a woman. So obviously she has decided to take a wife."

"How old's Antelope?" Cimarron asked.

"Her school record indicates that she has, in her words, 'seen thirteen summers.' "

Cimarron wondered about the reason for the anger that he suddenly felt stirring within him but he said nothing.

Neither did he say anything several days later when Antelope emerged from the lodge where she had been confined and once again let the scented smoke waft over her body that was still wrapped in a buffalo robe.

He watched, the anger red within him, as Warrior Woman's relatives appeared.

They placed Antelope on a blanket and then carried her to Warrior Woman's lodge. When the girl reappeared some time later her hair was once again braided and red dots had been painted on her cheeks. She was dressed splendidly now in a buckskin dress that was heavily beaded and around her shoulders she wore a brightly colored shawl. New moccasins were on her feet and horn rings adorned her fingers.

Cimarron thought she looked unhappy as she returned to her own lodge and to the feast that Walks with Wolves had prepared. When she caught sight of him standing alone, she beckoned to him and made signs indicating that he was to come and share the feast her father had prepared to celebrate her marriage to Warrior Woman.

As he walked toward the raucous celebration, he was aware of Warrior Woman's eyes watching him. He did not meet them. He sat cross-legged on the ground and tried to eat only to find that he had no appetite.

But he did not want to insult Walks with Wolves so he forced himself to eat whatever came to hand without tasting any of the food. Later, when his eyes locked on Antelope's, he saw with regret that hers were wet and her expression downcast.

5

Cimarron spent most of the morning following the marriage feast erecting a lodge of his own not far from Big Eagle's.

That afternoon, he decided it was time he did some scouting in the area to see whether he could turn up any sign of Jake Farley.

He left his bear claw necklace inside the lodge and, carrying his gear, set out for the spot near the camp where several young Cheyenne boys were grazing the tribe's pony herd. But he halted when he came to Warrior Woman's lodge and stood for a moment in silence watching Antelope, who was busily cleaning a buffalo hide.

Two other hides, already clean, were staked out on the ground, hair side down, with wooden pegs. Antelope, on her knees, was using a sharp blade that was lashed to an elkhorn handle to scrape the dried flesh from the hide. As Cimarron watched her, she switched to a stone scraper and then, when the hide was clean, she began to rub buffalo fat into it.

"Aren't you supposed to be in school?" he asked her.

She didn't look up at him but simply shook her head and began to squeeze the hide as she worked the fat deeper into it.

"I was told you went to school at the Agency."

"I did." She glanced at the rawhide rope that was suspended between two poles planted in the ground.

"I'll give you a hand," Cimarron volunteered.

Antelope looked up at him. "You would do the work of a woman?"

"I'll do whatever needs doing to help out a friend." He picked up the hide and draped it, skin side down, over the rawhide rope. As Antelope gripped one end of it, Cimarron gripped the other and they began to pull it back and forth across the rope to stretch it.

"Warrior Woman," he said, "didn't bring down but one buffalo during the hunt the other day. Where'd all those other hides come from?" He nodded in the direction of the mound of hides on the ground behind Antelope.

"From Trader Drake at the Agency."

"Warrior Woman bought them from him, did she?"

"No. He gave her these hides to tan and make into buffalo robes for him to sell."

"But she turned the job over to you."

"It is the work of a woman—a wife." Antelope's strong fingers began again to squeeze the hide to soften it. "Trader Drake gives Warrior Woman food for robes. We have very little."

"Well, I guess you're glad you don't have to go to school."

Antelope looked up at Cimarron. "I want to go to school!" she declared vehemently. "I want to learn. I want—"

She fell silent as Warrior Woman emerged from the lodge and glared first at her and then at Cimarron.

"She must work," Warrior Woman said to him. "Not talk."

Cimarron touched the brim of his hat to her and then nodded to Antelope before walking away from the lodge, his saddle slung over his shoulder.

When he reached the pony herd's grazing ground that was some distance from the camp he checked his horse's neck wound and grunted with satisfaction when he saw that it had begun to heal. He was about to saddle and bridle the animal when he noticed the skunk tail tied to the bay's tail with a thin piece of rawhide. He called to one of the boys who came over to him.

"You speak English?" he asked, and the boy nodded.

"Do you know who did this to my horse?"

The boy giggled and called out something in Cheyenne to the other boys who were guarding the herd.

"Who did it, boy?"

"Antelope," the boy answered. "She did it the day after you came to the reservation.

"Why'd she do it? You know?"

"Skunk is strong medicine. Chase minio and mistai away from man who rides horse that skunk protects."

70

"Minio? Mistai?"

The boy glanced fearfully about him. "Mistai are spirits that come in the night to frighten people. Maybe hurt them. Minio are spirits who live in water. Very bad spirits. They drag men down into water. Drown them."

"I'm much obliged to you for looking after my horse."

When the boy had gone, Cimarron saddled and bridled the bay and then, after flipping down the stirrups, stepped into the saddle and instead of riding out to search for Farley rode north to the Darlington Agency.

Not long after passing Fort Reno, he caught his first glimpse of the buildings of the Darlington Agency, which were scattered on the far bank of the Canadian River's north fork.

He forded the river, turned his horse, and when he reached the wide dirt road that intersected the one he was on, he glanced to his left and saw the two-story brick building in the distance that was, he realized, the school Antelope had attended before her marriage.

Behind him, Dr. Tolliver appeared in the doorway of his house, which was on the western corner of the street. "Cimarron!" he called out. He left the house and hurried up to where Cimarron had halted his horse. "I planned on coming down to have a look at you before now but, well, with one thing and another, I never got there. How are you feeling?"

Without giving Cimarron a chance to answer the question, Tolliver beckoned peremptorily, turned, and strode back into his house.

Cimarron dismounted and, leaving his horse with its reins trailing, followed Tolliver inside the house. He found the doctor in a room off the center hall.

"Come in, come in. This is my surgery as you can see. Now then. Let's have a look at you."

"I'm feeling fine, Doc."

"Drop your pants and take off your shirt."

Cimarron shrugged and did as he was told. With his jeans bunched around his boots and his shirt off but his hat still on, he waited patiently as Tolliver removed the bandages from his wounds.

"You've got a thoroughly battered body," Tolliver commented. "What's this?" He tapped a small mass of scar tissue in the middle of Cimarron's back.

"Horse took a notion to make a meal of me but I took a notion to change his mind. Did. With a quirt."

"And this?" Tolliver pointed to a livid welt on Cimarron's left buttock."

Cimarron smiled. "There was a lady, Doc. I met her up in Dodge City. She had a knife and when we had a falling out over something or other she used it on me."

"A doctor can read a patient's history by studying that patient's body. I'd say your history is, to say the least, a colorful one."

"You think maybe I'll live, Doc?"

"You'll live and you'll thrive too, with a constitution as strong as yours obviously is. I'd expected to find you still flat on your back once I got back to Big Eagle's lodge."

"I've been up and around. Even built my own lodge today. It's not far from Big Eagle's. War Pony gave me a hide to cover it with and Big Eagle lent me some cooking utensils."

"How is the old man?"

"Big Eagle? Fine as far as I can tell."

As Tolliver applied a thick coating of salve to Cimarron's wounds, he said, "Big Eagle has consumption. I've been doing my best for him but his age is against him. It's a sad fact but time eventually turns on all of us and becomes the enemy which in the end always defeats us." Tolliver took clean bandages from a glass case and began to cover Cimarron's wounds.

"Well," he said when he had finished his task, "there's nothing much more I can do for you, Cimarron. You can do as you please now although I don't know why I bother to tell you that since you've been building a tepee and riding your horse and doing heaven only knows what else out there on the reservation since I first treated you."

"It's that 'heaven only knows what else' part, Doc, that will put the finishing touches on my cure."

"I'm sure it will if you're able to practice it," Tolliver declared heartily, matching Cimarron's grin.

Once outside the doctor's house, Cimarron freed his horse and, leading it, cut diagonally across the street, where he tied its reins to the hitch rail in front of the squat building, which had a painted sign nailed above its door: Drake's Trading House.

He went inside the building, a bell above the door tinkling

as he did so, and stopped short when he saw the woman behind the plank counter. He had been expecting to see a man—Drake himself or a male clerk—but the woman facing him, her elbows propped on the plank counter and her chin resting in her hands, was . . .

His eyes dropped to her pendulous breasts, which rested on the counter, and the deep cleavage between them, which was revealed by her low-cut blouse. Hefty, he thought. A handful, he thought. Not pretty and not all that young anymore either. But not to be ignored. Hair the color of not-yet-ripe corn. Eyes—were they gray? Smoky, he decided. Nice lips.

"Yes, sir?"

Cimarron went up to the counter and, when the woman straightened up, he realized she was almost as tall as he was.

"You're the lawman who's living on the reservation," she said, her hands on her hips as she studied him.

"Now how'd you know that?"

"Heard talk about you. Heard you were raw-boned and rugged looking. You fit the description. Besides, I know all the white men around here and I've never seen you before so—" She let her words trail away.

"My name's Cimarron."

"I know that too. Mine's Loretta. Loretta Croft. Well, what can I do for you today, Cimarron?"

He didn't dare tell her but he thought she could damn well do it for him every day and at least twice on Sundays. "I'm here to buy some flour. Some corn."

"Sounds like you're setting up housekeeping on the reservation with the rest of the bucks."

"How much a pound for the flour and the corn?"

Loretta quoted him a price and he whistled through his teeth. "Steep," he remarked, reaching into his jeans. "But my friends are in need and I'm able to help them out so—"

"You're not buying for yourself?"

"Nope. For a girl—a woman I know on the reservation."

"An Indian?"

Cimarron nodded and withdrew his money from his pocket.

"The price is double for Indians."

He met Loretta's steady gaze and nodded. "So that's the lay of the land, is it? You got a white price and a red price."

"I don't make the prices. Drake does."

"He here?"

Loretta shook her head.

"Well, now, Miss Croft, you can see that I'm a white man so it seems to me I ought to be able to buy at your white price."

"You're buying for Indians you said and I don't dicker."

"I do. But maybe I'd better do my dickering with Agent Tracy. Does he know how you run this establishment?"

"He ought to. He let the contract for this place to Drake. Him and Drake are partners."

Cimarron considered that information. "Where do you fit in?"

"Did you come here to hear my life story or to buy supplies?"

"I wouldn't mind listening to your life story, Miss Croft, but right now I'm here to buy."

"And I'm here to sell. How many pounds do you want of each?"

"Ten."

Loretta turned her back to him and pulled open the tin bin behind her. "Dammit," she muttered. "Wait a minute. I'll be right back." She walked the length of the counter and then disappeared through a rear door. She was back several minutes later dragging a huge sack of flour along the wooden floor.

"I'll give you a hand with that," Cimarron volunteered.

"No need. I can manage."

But he was already behind the counter and taking the sack from her. He hauled it over to the open bin, pulled the string to open it, and then dumped its contents into the bin. He waved the rising clouds of flour away and then handed the sack to Loretta. As he did so, he caught a glimpse of the letters stencilled in black on the sack: U.S.

"You do a brisk business here, do you?" he inquired offhandedly as Loretta took the sack from him and tossed it out of sight under the counter.

"We do all right." She picked up a metal scoop from the shelf behind the counter and began to fill a paper sack with flour, which she had placed on the scale.

"There's no need for you to hold the scale steady," Cimarron said. "The sack won't tip."

Loretta removed her thumb from the scale, closed the sack, and handed it to him. She began to measure out corn which

74

was stored in a bin next to the flour. This time her thumb never touched the scale.

"Much obliged," Cimarron said as he paid her and scooped up his two sacks.

Once outside, he placed his two sacks in his saddlebags and untethered his horse. After stepping into the saddle, he started back the way he had come, but before he reached the camp a dull throbbing sound reached his ear, rolling out over the empty land. Thunder? He looked up at the sky but it was clear and glazed with clouds crimsoned by the vanished sun. He strained his ears but heard nothing for a moment and then there it was again. Not thunder. A kettledrum. He turned his head and scanned the plain. There was no one in sight.

The low drumming continued and Cimarron's eyes were drawn to a stand of scrub oak in the distance. Curious, he angled his horse toward it and, as he neared the twisted and almost leafless trees, the drumming grew louder as if the drummer had been emboldened by the swiftly falling darkness.

A man stepped out of the trees and held up a hand.

Cimarron drew rein.

Nine Fingers gestured to the south.

"I was heading home, yes," Cimarron said. "Heard something."

"You heard the sacred drum," Nine Fingers told him. "You go to your lodge now. It is best you not know what happens here."

His curiosity increasing by the minute, Cimarron smiled and asked, "What *is* happening here?"

Before Nine Fingers could answer, War Pony appeared beside him and, when he recognized Cimarron, said, "Let him come."

Nine Fingers turned and quickly disappeared among the trees.

War Pony beckoned to Cimarron, who got out of the saddle and led his bay up to the nearest tree to which he tethered it. Then, bending low, he followed War Pony in among the trees until they came to a lone lodge that was unlike any Cimarron had ever seen before.

It had no flap and almost a third of it was open to the air and the night. Inside it, a small fire—not much more than a few coals—burned.

"You will not speak of what you see here tonight." War

Pony might have been giving an order or asking a question. He entered the lodge, beckoned to Cimarron, who stepped inside it, and then he sat down.

Cimarron sat down beside him, folding his legs under him as War Pony had done and glancing around at the faces of the men gathered around the fire. He recognized only Nine Fingers and Big Eagle. His gaze wandered along the line of containers that were made of clay, metal, and bark and which contained various foodstuffs, all of them carefully aligned in front of the crescent-shaped clay altar at the rear of the lodge.

Big Eagle raised a hand and shook a gourd rattle several times. In his other hand was a beaded and feathered fan, which he waved.

The drumming continued but the drummer and his drum were hidden from Cimarron's sight.

"Peyote ceremony," he whispered to War Pony, who nodded. "They let you get away with this?" he asked, and War Pony shook his head as the pebbles of the gourd on the end of its long stick rattled in Big Eagle's hand.

Nine Fingers began to sing in a low voice, a rhythmic chant that was quickly taken up by several of the other seated men. The drumming intensified. Big Eagle's gourd rattled loudly. A Cheyenne Cimarron had never seen before gestured with his two-piece peyote staff to which blue beads and brown feathers were attached.

Something, Cimarron noticed was being passed from hand to hand. War Pony received it, took something from it, and passed it on to Cimarron, who reached into it and came up with several small lumps about the size of radishes. He looked down at the peyote buttons in his hand and then passed the fringed buckskin pouch on to the man on his other side.

"War Pony," he whispered, "I've heard it told that these things can drive a man loco."

"They free our minds to see Heammawihio and Aktunowihio."

"You're saying this is some kind of religious service?"

War Pony nodded and began to chew on a peyote button. "You white men go to church house. This is our church house."

"But we don't drink red-eye whiskey when we go to our church houses."

"Maybe white men should. Then, like Cheyennes who chew peyote, they not sit down and talk *about* God. They do like us. They talk *to* the spirits."

Cimarron looked down at the peyote buttons in his hand. It's nothing but the above-ground part of the peyote cactus, he thought. I've seen them down in Mexico. Now, how'd these gents get their hands on them, he wondered.

War Pony glanced at him.

Cimarron shrugged and placed one of the buttons in his mouth and began to chew. He almost spat it out at once because of its bitter taste but he was aware that War Pony was still watching him, so he continued chewing, his eyes beginning to water.

The drumming ceased. So did the soft chanting. Silence came to the lodge and the only thing that moved within it was the smoke rising from the fire near the altar.

Cimarron swallowed and went on chewing.

Big Eagle solemnly chewed, swallowed, closed his eyes, and began to speak in a low steady voice. His words droned on and on and Cimarron was aware that several of the men were nodding as if in agreement as they watched him, War Pony among them.

"What's he saying?" Cimarron asked War Pony, suddenly feeling giddy.

War Pony didn't answer immediately but when, a moment later, he did, his voice was different, Cimarron realized. Not as harsh as usual. Soft. Cimarron was reminded of creek water bubbling over worn stones and then he was seeing War Pony's voice flowing between banks that were thick with tall rushes and he was not the least bit surprised at the wet and silvery words that were splashing up and into his ears.

"In the north there are still buffalo," War Pony translated as Big Eagle went on speaking. "Big buffalo. Heammawihio says he sees them and he cannot count them because there are so many. He says they wait for us. He says they cry out to us to come and kill them so that our people may live . . . Aktunowihio, the Wise One Below, wants his children to live and says we must go away from this evil place to where there is no sickness so our sons can grow strong and become warriors . . . give up the white man's beef and ways—let us lose the corn and become warriors once more . . ."

Cimarron's eyes widened as a volcano thrust itself up in

77

front of him and erupted in geysers of yellow fire and blue stars. He put out his hand and caught one of the stars and held it in both hands, so cold, so bright, so . . .

". . . whiskey and the ruin of our women are the white man's gifts to us," said War Pony, whose voice Cimarron now realized was not water but a warm fire he could see blazing forth from the man's lips.

The star in his hands melted and was gone and then, as he chewed another peyote button, he felt himself drifting up and away and time stretched out around him, a field full of dazzling flowers that he picked and decked about the neck, in scented garlands, of the naked nameless woman who soared beside him in the sky that smelled so starry.

The moon shook its rattle at him and he laughed and then the woman laughed as Big Eagle, on earth, went on praying to Heammawihio and Aktunowihio and he heard the Wise One Above and the Wise One Below both tell Big Eagle that the people must leave the reservation and go north to where the buffalo waited for them and white man's sicknesses would no longer torment them.

The woman beside him reached out to him and he reached out to her and the two of them exploded in a bright blue blaze and then, in fragments, drifted lazily back down to earth.

The drum sounded, pounding in Cimarron's ears. The rattle shattered his skull. He was blind now and drowning in the sheets of brilliant color only blind men, he knew, could ever hope to see. Every part of his body, every muscle, every bone, every cell throbbed. He was the drum, and the music he made *thrummed* in his mind and in the air and War Pony danced to it, a solemn dance, a mournful dance, until finally War Pony threw up his arms, renouncing the music, and rejecting the misery that was the white yoke on the red oxen, and freedom came spilling down from the skies and Cimarron saw them all marching, the men and women who were Cheyenne Nation, through the soft clouds, the smiling sun and moon their companions, as they went streaming north in search of freedom.

Then a golden haze settled on Cimarron and he saw Heammawihio, old and venerable and sad, and Aktunowihio, as aged and as morose, seated in it and the men were speaking without moving their lips and Cimarron willingly made the promise the Wise One Above and the Wise One Below had asked him to make. Sacred it was and without words was it made, but instead inscribed in the sky in a silence that was reverent.

Colors he had never heard swirled around Cimarron. Sounds he had never seen before assaulted his ears.

Someone was speaking to him but Heammawihio was gone. Someone was touching him but Aktunowihio had vanished.

"Eat," the someone said, and placed a bowl in Cimarron's hands.

He took it and ate, not knowing what it was that he consumed, knowing only that time had tricked him because now it was dawn and the day's first gray light was filtering down through the trees.

He ate ravenously as he became aware of the hunger that gnawed within him and as he ate he saw that the other men in the lodge were doing the same. Silence shrouded them all. The kettledrum was silent. Big Eagle's gourd rattle had disappeared.

When the men had finished eating, some of them began to gather up the altar and the bowls that had been aligned with it. Others folded the hide cover of the lodge and struck its poles. Ponies were brought and men mounted them and rode away, still silent.

"We go now," War Pony said.

Cimarron got to his feet and went to his bay. Moments later, he was riding beside War Pony as both men headed back to the camp that lay due south of them.

"That was some night," Cimarron ventured tentatively, shaking his head. "I don't know which of what happened was real and which wasn't."

"You were afraid?"

"No. I felt more like I was—this is going to sound a little silly, War Pony—but I felt like you and me and all the other men in the lodge were one and the same."

"Spirits come and it is so."

"I felt—I feel like I learned something only what I learned I can't find the words for. It's more of a feeling. A feeling that there's something I've got to do only the puzzling thing is I'm not sure what it is."

"You will know when it is time to know."

"I saw the Cheyennes moving north. Or at least I think I did."

War Pony nodded.

"I felt like I was traveling with them but at the same time I seemed to be watching them from far away."

War Pony was silent.

"Did Big Eagle—somebody—talk about jumping the reservation? Or am I making that up—imagining it?"

There was a loud report and at first Cimarron didn't recognize it as the sound of a shot, but then, as War Pony let out a yell and went galloping south, he saw the dust in the distance and went riding hard after War Pony toward the mounted men who were emerging from it as they drove most of the Cheyennes' pony herd ahead of them.

Cimarron, as he rode, saw one of the boys who had been guarding the herd leap onto the back of a pony and set out in pursuit of the three thieves. He saw one of them swing a rifle and knock the boy from his pony.

He let out a yell of his own then as he recognized the man who had struck the boy. He spurred his horse and he rode swiftly toward Jake Farley who, when he saw Cimarron coming toward him, raised his rifle and fired at him.

6

Farley's shot missed because Cimarron bent forward, slid down the side of his horse, and hung onto its neck.

He swiftly regained the saddle and, turning the bay, rode to the right to come up on Farley from behind. He glanced over his shoulder and saw War Pony and several other Cheyennes riding at an angle toward the ponies that were leading the herd in its flight. As he began to gain ground on Farley, the man let out a yell and shouted a command, but it came too late. The ponies were being turned and turned sharply by the Cheyennes, with the result that those animals in the lead began to collide with those directly behind them.

Cimarron rode into the dust the herd had stirred up just as two shots rang out. Rifle shots, he thought. But the Cheyennes, he knew, were unarmed. He came out of the dust coughing and blinking, but he was able to make out his quarry not far ahead of him.

Farley and the two men riding with him, he realized, had given up any hope of making off with the ponies and now were intent only on escaping.

They're liable to make it too, he thought angrily. The Cheyennes've got their ponies and that's all they're concerned about and rightly so considering that they've got no guns to defend themselves with against Farley and those other two jaspers.

He pulled his rifle from the boot and, gripping his horse with his legs, raised it, aiming at Farley. He got off a shot which had been meant for Farley's horse but it missed as Farley suddenly veered to the northeast and the other riders with him did the same.

Cimarron, after turning his horse sharply, heeled it savagely and the bay shot forward. As he neared Farley, he fired again. This time Farley's horse screamed and then stumbled as it was hit. The animal slowed, shaking its head, and Cimarron cut in front of it, drew rein, and raised his rifle. But he didn't fire. Instead, he rode up to Farley whose rifle was still in his hands, which now were busy with his mount's reins in an effort to control the wounded and frightened animal. Cimarron fired again, this time to one side of the animal's head.

When it reared, he fired a third time.

The horse reared again, backing away from Cimarron on its hind legs. It lost its balance and went over backward, throwing Farley from the saddle.

Cimarron, his left hand gripping the reins of the bay, sat his saddle, his rifle trained on Farley, who was getting to his feet. "Drop it!" he ordered, but Farley merely glared at him as the horse he had been riding got to its feet and went racing away.

"Drop it! You don't and—"

Farley dropped his rifle.

"Now you and me," Cimarron told him, "we're going to head south to Fort Reno. I'm counting on the fact that they'll have a guardhouse there to keep you in till I get ready to take you back to Fort Smith. Circle around and let's get going."

As Farley came toward him with his hands above his head, Cimarron slowly wheeled his horse, intending to follow his prisoner once the man had moved past the bay.

But Farley suddenly halted and, in one swift movement, pulled at a cord around his neck and drew out the long-bladed knife that had been hanging from the cord and resting between his shoulder blades beneath his shirt.

"Drop it!" Cimarron shouted, his finger tightening on the trigger of his rifle.

Farley didn't. Instead, he slashed wildly at the bay's chest.

The horse, its eyes rolling wildly, stepped swiftly away from its attacker and then it bolted.

Cimarron, thrown off balance, lost his grip on the animal's reins and then, as the bay bucked and sunfished in its pain, he was thrown from the saddle. He fell, hitting the ground hard, and lost his grip on his rifle, but he swiftly sprang to his feet.

Farley stood with the rifle Cimarron had forced him to drop

once again in his hands and aimed now at Cimarron, who ran to his horse, which was circling and snapping in vain at the bloody wounds in its chest.

He threw himself behind the horse and held tightly to the saddle horn while pressing hard with his left shoulder against the agitated animal in an effort to steady it.

Farley fired.

The bay, hit, staggered against Cimarron. It tossed its head, its mane flying, and then it staggered again and Cimarron felt it falling.

He leaped backward as the animal toppled to the ground, narrowly missing him, and lay there thrashing helplessly. He dropped to the ground and scrambled crablike along it. He made a grab for his rifle but Farley got to it first and kicked it out of his reach.

He tried again to get his hands on his rifle and received a blow on the side of the head from Farley's heavy boot that momentarily stunned him. He looked up as he got to his hands and knees and saw Farley staring down at him and grinning, the man's glittering black eyes dancing with delight and his thin lips drawn back over his yellowed teeth in a parody of a smile.

Cimarron stiffened as he saw the two men who had been riding with Farley come galloping toward them. He threw himself forward, belly down on the ground, and then came up under Farley's rifle barrel, knocking the gun from the man's hand.

A shot zinged past him and he made a grab for Farley, intending to use him as a shield against the riders who were upon them now, but Farley kneed him in the groin and, as he bent over in pain, the stock of a rifle wielded by one of the mounted men slammed against the base of his skull and he went down.

"Come on!" he heard one of the riders yell, and he heard Farley's roar of protest. He turned and looked up, reaching for his .44, as Farley was hauled up behind one of the two men who then wheeled his horse and galloped back the way he had come, followed by the other rider.

Cimarron, both hands on the butt of his .44, fired into the dust the riders were raising and saw with disappointment as it began to settle that he had missed and that the three men were now out of range as they rode north.

He got to his feet, holstered his revolver, retrieved his rifle, and raced for his bay, intending to set out in pursuit of Farley but, when he reached the horse, he knew that he would never again mount the animal.

The horse was lying on its right side, its legs kicking, its body seized and shaken by sudden spasms. Blood and saliva dripped from its mouth, which the bit had torn. Blood flowed freely from the knife wounds in its chest and pulsed from the bullet hole near its shoulder.

Cimarron glanced into the distance where Farley and the others were now almost invisible, and then raised his rifle. He took careful aim at the horse's head and then squeezed the trigger.

The horse gave one final shudder before exhaling noisily and then lying motionless at his feet.

He knelt and began to strip his gear from the dead animal, swearing silently as he did so. Moments later, carrying it and his rifle, he set out for the long walk back to the camp of the Cheyennes and his lodge.

Cimarron arrived at the camp in the late afternoon and, after stowing his gear in his lodge, took the flour and corn from his saddlebags and made his way to Warrior Woman's lodge where he found Antelope outside it working on one of the buffalo robes.

She looked up at him as he dropped his gear at his feet, removed the sacks of flour and corn from his saddlebags, and held them out to her.

"Go on, take them," he said. "I got them for you. For you and Warrior Woman."

"Warrior Woman will not take her share of the Agency beef. She says we must provide for ourselves."

"Now that's a real admirable way for her to feel," Cimarron commented, stifling the anger that Antelope's reticence had aroused in him. "But you told me you didn't have enough food. There's corn in this sack." He held it up. "Flour's in this one." He held up the other sack and then placed them both on the ground in front of Antelope as someone behind him gave an angry shout.

He turned to find a crowd of Cheyennes gathering around a white man he immediately recognized as Enoch Tracy. Tracy held up his hands to silence the Indians, but they continued to mutter among themselves, darting occasional hostile glances in Tracy's direction.

Cimarron strode over to the gathering and stood, his thumbs hooked in his cartridge belt, on its edge.

War Pony, he saw, was among the crowd and he listened as the man took a step toward Tracy and said, "We need more food. The beef ration—already gone. We have no flour. No corn. Only coffee and salt."

"Feed us!" Walks with Wolves shouted angrily, and Cimarron winced as he continued to stare at the dependent men who had once been brave warriors and skillful hunters.

"Give us ammunition!" another man shouted.

Tracy shook his head. "I have received orders today from Major Linnett at Fort Reno. One of his troops was returning to the fort from patrol duty last night and they reported to him that some of you were holding the forbidden peyote ceremony. He notified the Central Superintendency and the result is as I've just explained. No ammunition will be issued."

"How can we hunt if we have no—" Nine Fingers asked, his dark eyes flashing.

"You can't," Tracy answered, interrupting him. "That, I gather, is the point of the order to refuse you ammunition. Major Linnett and the officials of the Central Superintendency are well aware that the revival of the peyote ceremony has been in the past the precursor of flights from the reservation."

Cimarron shouldered his way through the throng and, when he was facing Tracy, his thumbs still in his cartridge belt and his stance deceptively relaxed, he asked, "What's their religion got to do with reservation jumping, Tracy?"

"Religion!" Tracy barked. "Drugs have nothing to do with religion! They do have to do with discontent and ill-considered actions. These dreamers can be dangerous. Believe me, I know what I'm talking about."

"Dreamers can be dangerous," Cimarron agreed mildly. "I mean if I dreamed I could fly and I jumped off a barn roof to make my dream come true—well, I might find myself in more trouble than Adam did after eating that apple."

"My point exactly," Tracy remarked smugly, and started to turn away.

"Hold it a minute, Tracy. You go and take a man's dream away from him—well, a man without a dream might turn out

85

to be even more dangerous than one with a head chock full of them. Dreams are just hopes going under another name. You kill one, you kill the other and what you've got left is misery. Now misery's a funny thing. It can make a man do things he wouldn't ever think of doing when his belly's even half-full and his head's stuffed full of hope concerning what tomorrow might bring him.''

"I am under orders," Tracy practically shouted. "No ammunition! And no one is allowed to leave the reservation for any reason—hunting very much included.''

"But you got yourself money to pay for provisions if you could get your hands on them, I reckon," Cimarron prodded.

"I do. I have my allotment. But the next annuity shipment is not due for another week and I've been unable to buy any more cattle so—''

"If I got you provisions, you'd pay for them?''

"Certainly I would but—''

Cimarron turned and elbowed his way through the crowd. He rounded it until he had reached War Pony. "I had to shoot my horse. I'd like to borrow one of your ponies.''

"Come.''

Cimarron followed War Pony to where the herd was again grazing under the watchful eyes of the several young boys who had been guarding it previously.

"Take one," War Pony said, pointing at the ponies.

Cimarron walked in among them, avoiding the pintos and examining a dun and a black that had caught his eye. The dun, he discovered, had a shallow chest, which meant poor wind, but the black looked solid and it was long-legged. As he ran his hands lightly over the animal's body, it turned its head and tried to bite him. He's still got spirit to spare. He thought. His mustang's blood's not altogether cooled. He's short, maybe thirteen hands high, but I can tuck my boots up alongside his ribs so they won't drag if I have to.

'I'll take this black,'' he called out to War Pony, "if that suits you.''

War Pony nodded and left to rejoin the crowd that was still clustered around Tracy.

Cimarron, as he headed back to his lodge, heard a cry that he was sure had come from Warrior Woman's lodge. He looked in that direction and saw Antelope run from the lodge with Warrior Woman right behind her, a birch switch in her hand.

She brought it down several times on Antelope's back and bare legs and Antelope, dodging frantically in an effort to avoid the vicious blows, cried out in pain.

Cimarron ran up to the two women and ripped the switch from Warrior Woman's hand. He threw it on the ground and stood facing her as she shouted in Cheyenne at him, her hands clenched into fists at her sides. He ducked as she suddenly swung a fist at him and then he blocked her next attempt to hit him by raising his right forearm.

She turned, furious, and ducked under her lodge flap, reappearing a moment later carrying the sacks of flour and corn which she hurled at Cimarron.

They struck his chest and fell to the ground where they both burst, spilling their contents over his boots.

Cimarron turned and stalked through the camp while, behind him, Warrior Woman screeched in Cheyenne and shook her fists at him.

Once inside his lodge, he gathered up his saddle, bridle, rifle, and other gear, a smile parting his lips as the sound of Warrior Woman still screeching in the distance assaulted his ears. He tossed his saddle over his shoulder and was about to leave the lodge when he thought he caught movement out of the corner of his eye. He halted and looked around. What had he seen? Had he seen anything?

His buffalo robe that was lying on the ground at the rear of the lodge moved. He stared at it, drawing his .44. "I've got you spotted," he said sharply. "Come on out from under there."

The buffalo robe was still now.

Cimarron strode to it and jerked it up and away.

Antelope, huddled on the ground with her arms wrapped around her body, stared silently up at him.

"Well, I'll be damned!" he exclaimed and holstered his gun. "I reckon I know why you hid out but what I don't know is why you hid out here. Why didn't you go home to your daddy?"

"Walks with Wolves would send me back to her. She paid him five ponies for me." Antelope sat up, her eyes still on Cimarron.

"That's a point now, isn't it? Tell you what. You hide out

in here as long as you want. Me, I've got to ride out after a horse thief. Maybe by the time I get back you and Warrior Woman'll have settled your domestic dispute, which I'm real sorry I was the cause of.'' Cimarron turned his back and reached for the lodge flap.

Antelope leaped to her feet and sprang at him. She landed on his back and her arms went around his chest. Her legs went around his thighs.

"Whoa!" he yelled in surprise, his saddle sliding from his shoulder to the ground. He tried to dislodge her hands, but they were clasped tightly and he failed to do so. He dropped the rest of his gear and went to work on her hands with both of his own and finally dislodged them. But before he could free himself of her legs, she was frantically grasping his groin, and his hands, which had been tearing at her ankles, slid up her thighs.

"Whoa!" he repeated, this time to himself. "You're a married lady, Antelope, and this is not how you ought to behave out of your—" he searched for the right word— "spouse's sight.''

"I don't want a woman. I want a man. I want *you!*" Antelope suddenly released him and then circled him until she was standing in front of him looking up into his eyes, her hand gently stroking him.

"But you're just a child!" Cimarron protested.

"I have become a woman.''

"Well, yes, I know all about that but—listen to me, honey. I can understand how you feel," he told her, conscious of the rapid hardening of his flesh as Antelope continued to stroke and squeeze him. "But you Cheyenne women have a reputation for being chaste and what you're doing—well, it's not near to chaste.''

Antelope began to unbuckle his cartridge belt. She placed it on the ground and then began to unbutton his shirt.

"You oughtn't to—''

She had his shirt off and was working on the buttons of his jeans.

"I ought to—''

"Sit,'' she commanded and, when Cimarron didn't, she put her hands on his shoulders and he let himself be forced down until he was sitting on the ground. She pulled off his boots. Then, his jeans.

She knelt down and her tongue flicked along the length of him. Then, straightening, she pulled off her buckskin dress and tossed it aside.

Cimarron stared in surprise at the leather belt that was tied around her waist, knotted in front, and which wound-down between her thighs. Chastity belt, he thought. Warrior Woman's doing, he thought.

Antelope bent down and pulled his knife from his boot. She sliced the belt's leather thongs and threw it to the ground. Then, as Cimarron got to his feet, she took him by the hand and led him to the buffalo robe. She gave him a sudden shove which sent him sprawling upon it.

He rolled over, staring up at her small breasts, and letting his eyes roam down the gentle curves of her young body.

Her legs were slender but strong. Her belly was flat and, as she ran her fingers seductively over it and then down to cover her mound, Cimarron groaned with desire.

As if his groan had been a signal of some kind, Antelope dropped down beside him and her body, every part of it, became a whirlwind of motion. Her hands were upon him—here, there—and her body was pressing against him, her legs entwining themselves around him as she went about arousing him.

His hands tried to seize her but she eluded his grasp. Her tongue was on him and then her legs were rubbing against him as he throbbed with lust for her.

He rose and she was beneath him, her fingers delicately flicking over his back, along his thighs, across his buttocks.

He plunged within her and, as she cried out, he realized she was—had been a virgin. She shuddered beneath him and he remained motionless until her spasms ended.

"I'm real sorry, honey," he whispered but could say no more because she pressed her lips against his, her tongue finding its way into his mouth. Then his tongue was within her mouth and her pelvis lurched upward and he was thrusting hard—long, rapid strokes.

Antelope began to grunt, her eyes tightly shut.

He slowed his movements and raised his head to look down at her. Her mouth was open and she was sweating. He turned on his side, still within her, and then turned her and turned again until she was astride him, looking down at him and moaning softly.

He pulled her down until she had taken all of him and then he lifted her slightly. It took her only seconds to understand and then she was in control, her back arched over his legs, her hands braced on his knees, her head thrown back, and her braids tickling Cimarron's thighs.

She rose. Descended. Rose again.

Cimarron sighed, his neck arching backward.

Antelope opened her eyes and watched him as his hands rose and cupped her small breasts. As his thumbs manipulated her nipples, she swiveled her hips, rising and falling, still watching him and, every time he was about to explode within her, she changed or slowed her rhythm until he was teetering in ecstasy on a sexual precipice that soared toward the sky.

He whispered, "Please, honey."

Antelope slammed down against his pelvis and he erupted within her. His arms seized her and pulled her down on top of him.

"Good," she murmured, her cheek against his chest.

He wasn't sure if she had been telling him it had been good or if she had been asking him if it had been good. "Good," he repeated, still stiff inside her.

A screech.

Warrior Woman, he thought drowsily, dreamily. She's still raising hell out there.

But Warrior Woman was standing inside his lodge, the lodge flap clutched in one hand, the other fisted and thrust toward him.

Antelope cried out and withdrew from Cimarron.

He turned his head and saw Warrior Woman. He let out a yell and sprang to his feet, wrapping the buffalo robe around him.

Warrior Woman disappeared. Outside the lodge, she continued screeching at the top of her voice while slapping her hands against the lodge covering.

Cimarron, as he hurriedly dressed, heard other voices outside the lodge now, the voices of both men and women. He dressed quickly, pulled on his boots and ordered Antelope to dress, which she quickly did, fear twisting her features.

He strapped on his cartridge belt and left the lodge after warning Antelope to be silent by pressing a finger against his lips.

Warrior Woman was addressing the crowd that had gathered in the center of the camp. She turned and, when she saw Cimarron, she gave a wild cry and pointed at him.

Antelope came out of the lodge to stand beside him.

Warrior Woman screamed again, pointing this time to Antelope, who ducked behind Cimarron. Then she barked a command and a man on the edge of the crowd placed a kettledrum on the ground and began to beat upon it.

Warrior Woman picked up a stick that had been lying on the ground and began to dance.

"What's she got to dance about?" Cimarron wondered aloud, puzzled.

"She dances the Omaha dance," Antelope whispered to him.

"What's that?"

"She dances to send me away from her lodge."

Warrior Woman danced up to the drum and the drummer's hands withdrew from it. She struck it a mighty blow, threw the stick in her hand toward a group of leering men, and shouted something in the Cheyenne language.

"What'd she say?" Cimarron asked.

"There goes my wife," Antelope translated. "I throw her away. Whoever gets that stick may have her!"

The men dodged the stick, grinning, as Warrior Woman stalked angrily back to her lodge.

"You'd best go back to your daddy's lodge, honey," Cimarron advised Antelope.

She shook her head. "He will not have me now. He will be ashamed of me."

"Then you stay in my lodge. Once I get back, we'll figure out what to do about you."

As the crowd began to disperse, Cimarron entered his lodge, gathered up his gear, and then left the lodge and quickly made his way to the spot where the pony herd was grazing.

When he reached it, he found War Pony and Nine Fingers moving about in the herd and, as he watched them, War Pony indicated two of the animals which Nine Fingers led out of the herd by ropes he looped about the ponies' necks.

Cimarron went up to War Pony and said, "Looks like you're going to do some riding."

War Pony said nothing. He took his knife from his waistband and went up to the chestnut that Nine Fingers had cut from the herd. He gripped the rope around the pony's neck, raised his knife, and slashed the animal's throat. He maintained his hold on the rope as the pony reared and blood geysered from its severed jugular vein to spray his naked chest and face.

Cimarron watched in silence as the chestnut's legs gave way and it fell to the ground, blood still spurting from its savaged neck.

War Pony went over to the other animal, which was struggling to break free of Nine Fingers as it caught the scent of the dying pony's blood. He repeated the process with the second animal and then stepped back to watch it die.

"We have no bullets for our guns," he said without looking at Cimarron. "So we will have no buffalo meat for our bellies. The people starve."

Cimarron remained silent, feeling somehow responsible for the death of the two ponies. He knew he wasn't responsible but he knew he was white and a part of the white world that had issued its decrees—its destructive decrees—that had led to what War Pony had, in desperation, been forced to do.

As the butchering of the two dead animals began, Cimarron cut the black he had selected earlier out of the herd and threw his saddle blanket over the pony's back. He was aware of the silence of the two men behind him who were carving up the meat they and their families would later eat and he sadly recalled the excited and joyous banter of the Cheyennes following their earlier buffalo hunt.

He placed his stirrups on his saddle and then set the saddle on the black. It shifted position and pawed the ground with one foreleg.

"It's heavier than what you're used to," he told the black. "But you can manage it, I reckon." He checked the rigging straps and rings and then fastened the cordage cinch which caused the black to snort in protest and prance about. "Easy now." He patted the animal's neck and then worked his curb bit into its mouth. As the animal tossed its head, he slipped the split-ear headstall over the animal's ears.

After booting his rifle, he put a foot in the stirrup and was about to swing into the saddle when he heard his name called. He turned and found Enoch Tracy riding toward him.

"I heard what you did!" Tracy called out and then drew rein when he reached Cimarron.

"That Antelope's a lusty little thing," Cimarron said sheepishly. "I didn't mean to—but, well, it just sort of happened, you might say."

"What are you talking about, Cimarron?"

"What are *you* talking about, Tracy?"

"Those horse thieves you helped run off."

"Oh."

"They've been caught."

"By your Indian police?"

"No. They were arrested just north of the Kansas border and word was sent to the Central Superintendency when some ponies belonging to the Cheyennes and the Arapahos were found among the stock they were trying to sell. I just received word from Superintendent Manson that the thieves have been jailed in Dodge City."

"Was a man named Jake Farley one of those jailed?"

"Yes, he was one of the men captured."

"Well, I'm carrying a warrant for his arrest so I'd best get up to Dodge and try to pry him loose from the sheriff up there so he can stand trial in Fort Smith. First, though, I've got to ride over to Fort Reno to see what I can do about getting you some supplies."

"What do you hope to accomplish at Fort Reno?"

Cimarron swung into the saddle and, as the pony began to buck under him, he gave Tracy a wave instead of an answer to his question.

The black went bucking away from Tracy, and Cimarron, as it began to sunfish, hitting the ground hard each time as it came down, gripped the animal tightly with his knees to cut off its wind.

The tactic worked. The pony settled down, snorted twice, and then responded to Cimarron's tug on its reins.

He rode east and arrived at the haphazard cluster of buildings that was Fort Reno as the bugler was sounding Stable Call. Most of the buildings were built of planks and most had canvas roofs. There were rows of canvas tents on the northern perimeter and, Cimarron was pleased to see, one rude flat-roofed building in front of which a trooper patrolled that was obviously the guardhouse.

He imagined Farley's face peering through the single barred

window of the guardhouse and he began to smile. He was still smiling as he rode up to the narrow wooden building, which had a rudely lettered sign above its door announcing that it was the commandant's quarters.

He got out of the saddle and strode into the doorless building to find Lieutenant Kendrick sitting behind a table and making notes in a large ledger.

"I didn't expect to find you in here, Kendrick."

Kendrick looked up and smiled. "Cimarron, isn't it? Or does my memory fail me?"

"You got it, Kendrick. I came to talk to the commandant."

"Major Linnett is not on the post at the moment. In his absence, I am acting commandant. What can I do for you, Cimarron?"

"The Cheyennes on the reservation—"

"They've fled?"

"No, they—"

"But there's trouble?"

"If you'll quit jumping down my throat every time I open my mouth, Kendrick, I'll speak my piece." When Kendrick said nothing more, Cimarron continued, "There's trouble enough all right. Those Indians are sick and they're starving. Some of them are sick *because* they're starving. I'm here to lend Agent Tracy a hand. I want to requisition some stores from the fort's commissary."

"You're acting on behalf of Tracy?"

"I am."

"He authorized you to do so?"

"He did," Cimarron lied.

"Major Linnett wouldn't like it."

"What wouldn't he like?"

"Giving our supplies to the Indians."

"First off, you're not giving them. Tracy'll pay you for them and you can buy goods to replace what you send to the reservation. Second of all, I'm not asking you to clear your commissary's shelves and bins."

"What do you want?" Kendrick asked and, when Cimarron told him, he stroked his chin and murmured, "Rather irregular."

"So's dying of hunger when there's food to be found if a man knows how to go about finding it. Now, Kendrick, when you and me first met out on the trail, I figured you for a man

94

who'd do his best for the Cheyennes were he given half a chance. It looks to me like now you've got that half a chance. All you got to do is load up a wagon with the supplies and send it over to Darlington."

"You'll sign for the goods so that payment can be made?"

"I'll sign, yes."

Later, when the wagon was loaded, Kendrick prepared a bill of lading which Cimarron promptly signed and returned to him.

"You'll bring back the wagon?" Kendrick asked.

"Not me." Cimarron stepped into the black's saddle. "I'm not driving it. Order one of your troopers to drive it up and back."

Kendrick shook his head in chagrin. "You ought to be a military man, Cimarron. You do seem to like giving orders."

"You got it all wrong, Kendrick. I don't like giving orders. What I like is asking favors of a friend which I consider you to be."

Kendrick smiled and offered his hand, which Cimarron shook. "Where are you headed now?"

"Dodge City. There's a horse thief sitting in the jail up there that I'm bound and determined to get my hands on."

7

Three days later, Cimarron forded the Arkansas River and rode into Dodge. He was sweaty and he wanted a bath. He was thirsty and he wanted a drink. But the bath and the drink, he thought as he approached Front Street, would have to wait until he had seen the sheriff. So would the visit he planned to pay to Jessica.

He passed Wright and Beverly's store and, as cattle lowed in the pens behind him, he glanced at the entrance to the Long Branch Saloon two doors beyond Wright and Beverly's. Would she still be there? She might be. He hoped she would be but he knew that women like Jessica were restless creatures and, for all he knew, she might have moved on to Wichita or even Leavenworth.

The grating of a train's wheels on the rails in the Atchison, Topeka and Santa Fe yards on his right interrupted his reverie and he rode on, spurring the black lightly, until he reached the sheriff's office, where he dismounted and tethered the pony to the hitch rail.

He strode into the office and stood before the desk behind which a deputy was dozing. "You got a man named Jake Farley locked up in your jail," he stated. "I've come for him."

The deputy opened his eyes and squinted up at Cimarron. Suddenly, his eyes widened and he jabbed a finger in Cimarron's direction. "I know you. I remember you."

Cimarron pulled his badge from the pocket of his jeans and showed it to the deputy.

The deputy glanced at it and then up at Cimarron again. "You're a lawman now? *You?*" Incredulity sharpened the man's tone.

"I am. Now, I'd be obliged if—"

"You damn nearly tore this town apart—when was it? Couple or three years ago it was, wasn't it?"

"Deputy, I—"

"You got into a fracas over one of the saloon girls. I forget her name."

Jessica, Cimarron thought, remembering that wild and wonderful time.

"You damn near wiped Dodge City off the map that night. It took a whole bunch of us to subdue you and throw you into a cell. Now here you come pretty as you please pretending to be a lawman."

"I'm not pretending, Deputy. I've got a warrant for Farley." Cimarron pulled it from his pocket and showed it to the deputy. "This takes precedence over your charge. I'm taking Farley back to Fort Smith to stand trial. Now, if you'll get him out here, him and me we'll be going."

"Only the sheriff himself can give you custody of one of our prisoners."

"Where is he, the sheriff?"

"Home eating dinner."

"Where's he live? I'll go there."

"Won't do you any good."

Cimarron leaned over and braced his knuckles on the top of the deputy's desk. "Why won't it do me any good to go see the sheriff?"

"Because he can't turn Farley over to you."

"Why the hell not? You just said—"

"Now, don't go getting riled, Cimarron. That's still what you call yourself like you did that night you ripped and roared through Dodge?"

"God damn you, Deputy! I've rode all the way up here from the heart of Indian Territory and I don't intend to spend another minute—not one more second—listening to you bullshitting around the bush."

"Farley's not here!" the deputy exclaimed, pushing his chair away from the desk and from Cimarron.

"Not here?"

"You heard me, *Deputy*." The last word had been spoken with an odd mixture of scorn and awe.

"Where is Farley?"

"I couldn't tell you that. We had to let him go. The

prosecuting attorney couldn't find out who the horses Farley and the others stole belonged to.''

''You knew damned well that some of them belonged to the Cheyennes and Arapahos!''

''I mean the other ones. The thieves had brand-blotted them so skillful that we couldn't identify the original brands and so we couldn't find anybody to testify against the thieves.''

''The Indians who owned those horses could testify though. Why didn't you get them to come up here and sit in on the trial?''

''The sheriff tried to do just that only Superintendent Manson up in Leavenworth wouldn't spend any money to send any redskin witnesses up here. The case—well, there was no case as a result. So we had to let your man—all of them—go.''

''Sonofabitch!'' Cimarron muttered and straightened up.

As he started for the door, the deputy called out to him. ''If you have it in mind to do a little hell-raising while you're here in town, Cimarron, well, we got ourselves a whole lot of empty cells in the back.''

Cimarron went through the door and stood on the boardwalk seething with frustration. He turned swiftly and slammed the heel of his fist against the wall of the building behind him. Then, freeing his black, he led it down the street and tethered it in front of the Long Branch.

Once inside the saloon, he looked around, but Jessica was nowhere to be seen. He went up to the bar and asked the bar dog when she started work.

''She doesn't work here anymore,'' he replied. ''Jessica's gotten too good for us.''

''She's moved on, has she?'' Cimarron asked, his frustration growing.

''She works at the Varieties now. It just opened this year. It's giving us stiff competition, I can tell you. It's got gambling, dancing, fancy drinks, and women to take up to the rooms upstairs.''

Cimarron left the Long Branch and made his way along the boardwalk. He entered the first barber shop he came to, noting the rows of personalized shaving mugs in the rack that was hanging on the wall to his left.

''Yes, sir?'' asked one of the three barbers in the shop.

''I'll be wanting a shave and a haircut. But first I could use a bath and somebody to wash these clothes I'm wearing.''

"Certainly, sir," the barber said. "Right through that rear door. Two bits for the bath, two for the laundering."

Cimarron went through the door the barber had indicated and into the huge steamy room behind it. Minutes later, he had stripped and was climbing into a galvanized tub that an attendant had filled with water that had been heated on the wood-burning stove that stood at one end of the room. He took the bar of soap and stiff-bristled brush the man handed him and proceeded to scrub the grime from his body. He ducked his head into the water and then lathered his hair. After he had rinsed it, he noticed that the water in the tub had turned a dark gray, almost black.

After climbing out of the tub some time later, he took the towel the attendant handed him, draped it around his waist, and sat down on a bench to wait for his clothes to be washed and dried.

An image of Jessica cavorted in his mind.

Restless, he got up and went out into the barber shop again, ignoring the startled expression on the barbers' faces. "You don't get ladies in here, do you?" he asked.

The three barbers solemnly shook their heads in unison.

"Then I'll just climb up here—" he got into the center chair, "and you can give me that shave and haircut I mentioned before. Only don't cut my hair so close my ears'll feel the wind whistling round them and my neck'll be baked by the sun."

"Sir," began one of the barbers, "perhaps it would be best if you waited until you're quite fully clothed before—"

Cimarron picked up a striped sheet from one of the chairs. "I'll hide under this so's not to embarrass anybody." He draped it over him and the barber he had selected fastened it around his neck.

As the barber's long scissors snip-snapped and his fingers tilted Cimarron's head first one way and then the other, Cimarron studied the rows of mugs facing him, each set neatly in its niche in the wall rack. Mighty fancy, he thought.

All of them bore their owner's name lettered in gold on the white porcelain and, in addition, a realistic illustration indicating the owner's profession. One mug bore a picture of a coffin. Others displayed a caboose, a telegraph key, a printing press, and a drayman's wagon.

"You get to wait on most of the town's businessmen,

looks like," Cimarron commented, and the barber beamed at him as he continued working with his scissors.

"I take pride in my work and I find the more discriminating among the men in town appreciate that fact," the barber commented with obvious pride.

"I knew you were the man for me even though I'm not what you could call all that discriminating."

"You did? How did you know?"

Cimarron gestured at the rack. "One sure way to pick a good barber is to pick the one with the most mugs by his chair." He closed his eyes and, a little while later, felt the barber applying warm lather to the back of his neck and to his cheeks and chin. He heard the *strop-strop* of a straight razor being sharpened on the leather strap which hung from the barber chair.

He felt the razor glide along the back of his neck and then a wet towel wiping away the lather. A moment later, he felt the razor slide smoothly along his cheek and down his chin. As the barber continued to shave him, he thought of Jessica and it wasn't long before his sense of frustration ebbed and he began to look forward to meeting her again. It had been a long time but he hadn't forgotten her nor the things she could do to a man to make him glad he'd been born and gladder still that he'd been lucky enough to meet her.

When the barber had finished, Cimarron, as the man whipped the sheet away, got out of the chair and returned to the room at the rear of the shop.

Dusk had settled on Dodge City as Cimarron—shaved, shorn, wearing clean clothes, and smelling of toilet water— entered the Varieties.

He made his way to the Long Branch, freed his horse, and walked it to the livery stable where he arranged to have it fed and rubbed down.

"How long'll you be leaving him here?" the stableman asked.

"Overnight," Cimarron answered and added, thinking of Jessica, "if I'm lucky."

Later, as he entered the Varieties, he was momentarily overwhelmed by the size of the establishment. He found himself in a large rectangular room that was already filled with both men and women. At one end of the room, on a raised platform, a three-piece band was playing. Tables lined the walls and a solid mahogany bar was being presided over by a bar dog with slickly pomaded hair and a neatly clipped mustache. There were curtained windows set in each wall and a fast game of faro was being played in front of one of them while, on the opposite side of the room, a slow game of poker was in solemn progress.

He headed for the bar but found his passage blocked by a young woman wearing a low-necked dress, its bodice trimmed in lace. He took in her smile, her heart-shaped face, and her blond hair into which she had woven a frisette of artificial curls.

"Buy a lady a drink?" she asked, and patted Cimarron's cheek.

"Sure."

"I took you for a high roller right off, cowboy," she said, linking her arm in his as they moved toward the bar.

"You took me wrong. I'm here looking for—"

"Action?"

"For a lady by the name of Jessica."

"My name's Annie."

"What'll you have, Annie?"

"The same as always, George," Annie told the bar dog who took a bottle of French brandy from beneath the bar and poured some into a tiny glass which he handed to Annie before glancing questiongly at Cimarron.

"Beer," Cimarron said and, when he had a glass in his hand, he turned to Annie and asked, "Is Jessica here tonight?"

"Why do you want to talk about Jessica when you've got me?"

"Honey, I don't have nor do I want you, not meaning to be insulting. I'm intent on renewing an old acquaintanceship with Jessica."

Annie downed her brandy and set her glass down on the bar. "She always gets the good-looking ones," she declared angrily and then, shrugging her shoulders, suggested, "If you don't find her, I'll be around and ready for anything you are." She patted Cimarron's cheek again and then left him.

He leaned back against the bar and surveyed the room.

The music rose in volume and several couples began to dance. Annie, giggling, plopped herself into the lap of a man seated at one of the tables. A man and woman climbed the staircase to the second floor.

Cimarron watched them until they disappeared. He was about to look away when he saw her appear on the second-floor landing. He resisted the impulse to shout her name and wave wildly to her. He watched her start down the steps, admiring her trim figure and remembering what it had been like with her those long lusty nights that were years away now. Her red hair seemed to be a fire which dimmed the lamps in the room. Her pale skin was still flawless, her full lips still provocative, her lush breasts still promising, her green eyes still seductive and alluring.

Jessica paused as she reached the bottom of the stairs, one hand resting on the railing as she surveyed the room.

A shrill whistle suddenly split the air, causing the band to miss a beat.

Cimarron turned his head at the sound and saw Annie, still in the man's lap, two fingers between her teeth, whistle again. When she had caught Jessica's eye, she pointed at Cimarron.

Jessica turned her head and, when she saw him, her mouth opened to reveal even white teeth and her eyes widened in surprise. Her hand left the railing, and went to her chest.

And then, to Cimarron's delight, she was running toward him, elbowing gamblers and dancers out of her way, her eyes glowing.

"Hey!" he yelled as she threw herself into his arms. "Hey now, honey!"

"Cimarron!" she cried, her arms clasped around his neck as she gazed into his eyes. "Where the hell have you been all this time, you old rooster?"

"Here and there. How've you been, Jessica?" He bent and kissed her on the lips.

"I've missed you, mister, and that's a fact." She sighed. "Come on. Let's find somewhere to sit down." She led him to an empty table beyond the bar.

When they were both seated at it, she reached across it and took Cimarron's hands in hers. As she leaned toward

103

him, his eyes dropped to her breasts, which were partially bared by the square-necked green gown she was wearing.

"You're looking fit," he told her. "Real fine, in fact. It seems, looking at you now, that it was only yesterday we were together."

"It was almost three years ago!" she chided him. "I haven't met a man like you since."

"Most of us are built pretty much the same. Talk about the same. Think alike."

"No one's built quite like you, Cimarron, take it from a working woman who not only ought to know but does know. Sure, a lot of men talk like you but I've never met one with the same devilment in his eyes or staying power where it counts most, if you take my meaning. And simply nobody I've ever met reads books from which he gets such crazy ideas as you do."

"Crazy ideas? Me?"

"Remember the time you told me that everything in the whole wide world is made up of the same things—germs you called them."

"That's what Lucretius called them, honey, not me. But, yes, I remember saying that."

"Well, now, if that's not a crazy notion, I've never heard one before. How could a flower and a stone be made of the same things, germs or whatnot? Anybody can see they're altogether different."

"Just as one woman's different from another," Cimarron remarked, determined to steer the conversation back into the channel that suited him. "Some are pretty, some plain. Now, you take yourself—you are a soothing sight for these sore eyes of mine that like to have fallen right out of my head on account of all the trail dust that's been stinging them for so damned long."

"Oh, it's so *good* to see you again, Cimarron!" Jessica cried and squeezed both his hands. "When that boy Willy told me you'd told him to look me up, I almost threw the poor kid out of the Long Branch on his ear. It was you I longed for, not him who couldn't have been a day over fifteen. Why, he was so scared that time that I had all I could do to get it up for him and, once up, keep it up." Jessica dissolved in a fit of laughter.

"Willy?"

"Don't you remember? He said you had both been on a cattle drive together. It was two years ago. The spring of '76."

Cimarron suddenly remembered the young wrangler who had been on the drive with him. "So he did take my advice and look you up once he got up here to Dodge. I told him to warn you that he wasn't much more'n a colt."

"He did but he also said you said to tell me he was a colt who had bottom."

"Did he?"

"I don't want to talk about him. I want to talk about you and me."

"I'll buy you a drink."

"I don't want a drink. I want my head perfectly clear for—later."

"Later? Why not right now?"

"Come on then!" Jessica cried and jumped up from the table. She led Cimarron through the crowd and up the stairs. She hurried him down the hall and then into a room that opened off it.

As Cimarron closed the door behind him, Jessica went to the gilded mirror that hung above her dresser and began to unpin her hair. Speaking to Cimarron's image that was reflected in the mirror, she said, "Don't just stand there. Get undressed."

He did as he was told as Jessica slipped out of her dress and underthings, kicked off her shoes, and pulled off her stockings. As Cimarron sat down on the edge of the bed, she came over and sat down beside him, her long red hair bathing her white shoulders.

"You smell sweet," she murmured, nuzzling his neck. "Minty."

He was aware of her own scent, which was subtly sexual, entirely animal, and unmixed with any kind of toilet water or perfume. He got off the bed and, on his knees in front of her, bent his head until it was between her thighs and his tongue slid back and forth along her, gently probing.

He felt her hands come to rest on the back of his head and he felt her opening as his tongue continued probing her, and then she was ready for deeper strokes and he gave them to her. He heard her exhale breathily and he kept at it, raising his hands to her breasts, which he gently fondled.

"*Oohhh*," she moaned. "Cimarron," she whispered, and fell back on the bed.

He rose and then, reaching down, he put his arms around her waist and drew her to her feet. Clasping her tightly against his body, he slowly entered her until he had penetrated her completely. He kissed her lips, the lids of her closed eyes, and then the base of her throat.

His hands slid down over her buttocks and gripped her thighs. "Put your arms around my neck," he whispered, and when Jessica did, he lifted her feet off the floor. "Wrap your legs around mine."

When her legs were in place, he said, "Lean back a little bit." She did and he bent his head to suck both her nipples, one after the other.

"Oh!" she exclaimed. "I—"

He bent his knees and then he was sitting on the floor, Jessica still astride him. He released his hold on her thighs and leaned backward, propping himself up with his hands behind him on the floor. "Bend backward," he told her, and she did.

Then she raised her pelvis slightly and a moment later brought it down, taking all of him into her again. She repeated the same movements, her head thrown back and her neck arched.

Cimarron lay down with his back on the floor. He reached up and put his hands on her shoulders and drew her down to him so that he could kiss her again.

Jessica braced her hands on his upper arms and began to move her pelvis, first one way, then the other, and Cimarron felt the pressure of his impending explosion, but he willed himself to wait, letting the barriers fall only when he saw Jessica's face above him contort in ecstasy and her body convulse in several rapid spasms of pleasure.

An instant later, he thrust his pelvis up and erupted within her.

With a drawn-out moan, Jessica settled down on him, still shuddering. "In my business," she murmured, "most men just jump on me and a minute later it's all over." She got to her feet and stood looking down at Cimarron, who was smiling up at her, his body relaxed and his mind drifting lazily. "I know that's what they pay women like me for but I sure do wish a few of them were like you."

"Like me?"

"I wish they'd give some thought to pleasuring the woman they're with. It would pay off for them in the end too."

Cimarron got up and led Jessica to the bed. When she was lying on her back, her arms at her sides, he lay down beside her and took her ear lobe between his teeth and nipped it. He ran his tongue along her neck as his hand slid between her legs and he began to massage her.

She reached down and took his still stiff shaft in her hand and gently, almost imperceptibly, began to stroke it, her fingers feathery on it, sending tremors through him.

"I think it was three times," she said, "but I really wasn't counting."

"They were good?"

"The first one—just a jolt really. The second one—an upheaval. But the third time I came—there at the end—an earthquake." She sighed dreamily.

"I had a customer last week," she continued. "You could have taught him a trick or two. He wanted me to use a riding crop on him—oh, never mind about him. He was just one of the hazards of this business I've been in for what well may be too long."

"Well, I don't need a whipping to fire this gun of mine," Cimarron said as Jessica bent down and her lips closed around him. "You pull its trigger every damned time, honey."

He felt her thumbs pressing below the base of his shaft and her fingers circling it as she sucked, her tongue hot as it caressed him. "Honey, I think—I *know* I'm going to—"

Her thumbs and fingers squeezed the base of his shaft and he felt himself subsiding.

Jessica continued to suck, her tongue darting along him, and each time, just as he was ready to erupt, she manipulated him as she had done the first time and he was brought to a crescendo of passion that bordered on pain.

He moaned, his fists clenched at his sides, his head swimming.

She withdrew her hands but her lips remained locked around him. They slid down the length of him, up, then down again.

As he exploded, Jessica swallowed twice and only then released him. She nestled beside him, one hand resting on his chest, the other tucked beneath him.

He turned his head and kissed her on the cheek. "I hope to hell it won't be another three years before you and me—"

Jessica propped her head up on one elbow. "It better not be! Don't you dare let it be! Promise me you won't!"

"Honey, you know I can't promise you that. Especially not now."

"Why especially not now?"

"I've got a job now." He told her about it.

"A deputy marshal," she said when he finished speaking. "A heller like you?"

"Things change. So do people."

"Cimarron, it's so dangerous down there in Indian Territory." She cradled her head in the crook of his arm. "You could be killed."

"Almost was some days back by a horse thief I'm hunting. First Farley came gunning for me and then—"

"Farley," Jessica repeated, interrupting him. "Are you talking about Jake Farley?"

"I am," Cimarron answered, tensing. "You know him? Where he is?"

Jessica shook her head. "I don't know him personally, no. But my friend Mattie does."

"Mattie?"

"Don't you remember her? Blond. Big blue eyes. Young— she wasn't twenty when you met her three years ago. She's still working in the Long Branch. Says she likes a quieter place than this."

Cimarron's memory went racing back in time and he recalled the girl named Mattie he had met when he met Jessica for the first time three years earlier. Mattie, he remembered now, had jokingly promised to chloroform Jessica so that she could, as she had put it then, "have you all to myself."

"What's Mattie got to do with Jake Farley?" he inquired.

"Farley was in jail here in Dodge," Jessica began.

"I know all about that," he said, nodding impatiently. "Is Farley with Mattie now?"

"No. But he was with her and Mattie has reason to regret that she ever laid eyes on him."

"He's gone?"

"He left town after what he did to Mattie. Him and the men he was riding with, they had to because Mattie went to

Marshal Masterson and he would have locked Farley up if he hadn't turned tail and run."

"I'd like to talk to Mattie."

As Cimarron started to dress, Jessica said, "I'll go with you. I'm afraid that if I let you out of my sight you might disappear and the good Lord knows when, if ever, I'll see you again.

When they both were dressed several minutes later, they left Jessica's room and then the Varieties. When they reached the Long Branch, they went inside and found Mattie standing alone at one end of the bar.

Cimarron recognized her immediately and was surprised that he had forgotten her. She wasn't beautiful but she was unmistakably a woman—buxom, big-hipped, and openly seductive—the kind of woman he seldom forgot.

He made his way up to her, followed by Jessica who, when they reached her, said, "Mattie, you remember Cimarron."

Mattie gave him an appraising glance and then, recognizing him, she smiled and angrily stamped her foot. "Dammit!" she declared.

"What's wrong, Mattie?" he asked her.

"I forgot to bring my bottle of choloroform." She gave Jessica a withering glance and then, turning back to Cimarron, she put one hand beside her lips and, speaking in a loud theatrical voice which Jessica couldn't help hearing, said, "It's in my room. I'll get it. You hold her still and, once she's under it, I'll get under *you!*"

Cimarron laughed, forgetting for the moment why he had come to see Mattie. But then, remembering, he said, "Jessica tells me you know a man named Jake Farley."

Mattie swore vehemently. "If you look close," she said to Cimarron, "you can see beneath all this powder I've got on my face that my eyes are black and blue."

Cimarron made out the faint bruises beneath both of her eyes. "He hit you?"

"Among other things, yes."

"Mattie," Jessica said, "Cimarron's a lawman now." She quickly explained.

"You're going to arrest Farley for what he did to me?" Mattie asked Cimarron skeptically.

"He's wanted for stealing horses in the Nations," he told her. "I'm trying to run him to ground. I thought maybe he might have said something to you that you might remember which would help me to trail him.''

"He talked about his whoring mostly,'' Mattie said bitterly. "About how he'd plugged more women than any distiller ever did whiskey bottles, as he put it.''

Cimarron waited, hoping.

"He bragged a bit about how stealing ponies from the reservation Indians down in the Territory was as easy as killing a coon caught in a trap. He said that even if he ever did get caught up here in Kansas where him and the others sell the horses they steal it was highly unlikely that he'd land in jail for any length of time because nobody would show up to testify against him.''

"What else did he say, Mattie?'' Cimarron prompted when she fell silent and began to finger her puffy eyes.

"He said that before him and his boys were through stealing horses there'd be a stolen horse in every barn and stable between the Platte and Cimarron rivers.''

"That's all?''

"That's all I remember. Except that he said next time he came back to Dodge, which he figured would be real soon, he'd bring me a Cheyenne pony to ride. I told him I wouldn't come within a country mile of him ever again. I told him if he had plugging on his mind next time he came to town he could plug that pony he talked about giving me.'' Mattie erupted in delighted laughter.

"He specifically said a Cheyenne pony?''

"He did.''

Jessica glanced at Cimarron. "You're thinking he's headed back to the reservation to try to pull off another raid on the Indians' pony herd.''

"I am. Mattie, I do thank you kindly for the information.''

"What do I get in return?'' she snapped, feigning anger.

"I'll pay you,'' Cimarron said.

She reached out and pulled the hand he had shoved into his pocket from it. "I'll take my payment in services rendered. How about right now? My room's just upstairs.''

"Some other time, Mattie. You see Jessica and me—''

"Damn you, Jessica!'' Mattie bellowed, shaking a fist in her friend's face. Then, turning to Cimarron, she said, "We're going to make up a petition, Annie and me are. Every working girl in Dodge is going to sign it and we're going to present it to Marshal Ed Masterson and have him get his brother, Bat, who's sheriff of Ford County, and his brother, George, who's tending bar right this minute over at Varieties. We're going to see to it that the three of them run Jessica out of town on a rail as a public menace not to mention an economic threat to every last one of us. Then maybe us other girls will have a chance to get *our* hands on any prime beef like yourself that happens to wander into town before *she* can get *her* claws into it.''

Jessica, smiling, planted a kiss on Mattie's cheek and Mattie, still pretending anger, winked at Cimarron.

He took Jessica by the arm and, after thanking Mattie again, steered her to the door and through it.

Outside in the night, he took her in his arms and kissed her gently.

"It's goodbye again, isn't it, Cimarron?"

"I'm afraid it is, honey. I've got to go after Farley. But I'll be back this way someday and then you and me'll get together again.''

"I hope so."

"You can count on it." He kissed her again and then started walking toward the livery stable.

"Cimarron!" Jessica called after him.

He turned back to her.

"Don't send me any more colts named Willy even if they do have bottom. Come yourself. Will you do that?"

He touched the brim of his hat to her and gave her a slight bow. "I will, honey. I'll come on the run next time whether you're ready for me or not."

"I'll always be ready for you, Cimarron."

"That's a real kindly thing to say, honey. That's the kind of thought a man like me tucks under his blanket with him on cold nights to warm him all the way down to his toes.''

Jessica blew him a kiss just before he turned and moved deeper into the dark night.

8

Cimarron spent the night sleeping on the plain, his .44 unholstered beside him, while above him fireflies and stars tried in vain to brighten the night.

When he awoke, the fireflies and stars had both vanished and the first gray light that preceded the dawn filled the sky.

He stretched, threw off his blanket, shook it out, and then pulled on his boots. He got up, strapped on his cartridge belt, holstered his Colt, and, thinking warm thoughts of Jessica which helped to chase away the morning's slight chill, he removed the hobbles from his pony and led it down to a nearby creek to drink. He knelt beside it and scooped up water in both hands, drinking his fill before rising and leading the black back to where he had made camp the night before. He saddled and bridled the animal and, although it frisked a good deal and tried once to lie down and roll in the grass, which was damp with dew, he soon had it ready to ride.

He stepped into the saddle and headed south, maintaining a steady pace that fell short of a gallop so that he would be sure to get back to the reservation astride the black and not on foot as a result of having driven the animal too hard for too long.

He scanned the plain as he rode, hoping to catch sight of riders and hoping that one of them would turn out to be Jake Farley. He saw no riders but he did see some prairie turnips growing in the wheat grass. He drew rein and harvested them before remounting and eating them raw as he rode on.

The sun was up and approaching its meridian when he spotted the ranch house in the distance and the outbuildings clustered around and behind it. He turned his horse and headed toward it, thinking that if Farley had passed this way the men working the ranch would probably have seen him.

Thinking too that they might let him sit down with them to dinner.

He came up on the ranch house from the rear and, as he circled around it, he heard first the sound of voices—men's voices—and then the sound of laughter that seemed to him to be particularly joyless. As he rounded the corner of the house, he realized that the laughter was coming from the barn on his left.

"Halloo!" he called out. "Hallooo the barn!"

A moment later, the figure of a young man appeared in the barn doorway.

"I was riding by," Cimarron told him, noting the man's holstered six-gun. "Saw this place. Thought I'd stop."

The man turned his head and called out, "It's a drifter, Mr. Rumson."

Well now, Cimarron thought with wry amusement. So it's a drifter I am, is it? Wonder if this fellow is as quick to lend a man a helping hand as he is to pigeonhole him.

Another man, considerably older than the first and unarmed, appeared in the doorway. "I'm Rumson and this is my ranch. What do you want?"

"Dinner," Cimarron replied bluntly, deciding that it was best to play his cards straight and fast with the two obviously unfriendly men facing him. "I can pay," he added.

Both men silently appraised him for a moment before Rumson asked, "You got yourself a name?"

"Cimarron."

"Where you headed, Cimarron?" asked the other man.

"South."

"We're busy," Rumson said before turning and disappearing inside the barn.

"Mr. Rumson don't feel easy with drifters," said the man who had first appeared. "He'll be happy to see you drift right on out of here."

"Much obliged for your warm welcome," Cimarron said and turned his horse.

He had not ridden far when he heard a wordless yell from inside the barn and a man shout, "The bastard kicked me!"

Rumson's voice then: "Grab him. Don't let him get away!"

Cimarron headed back toward the barn and, when he reached it, rode around to one side of it. He leaped from the saddle, leaving the black with its reins trailing as he flattened his back against the wall of the barn and, unholstering his .44, eased around to the front of the building and then on to its open door.

He heard the low voices of men talking inside and then the rumble of low laughter. How many men were inside the barn, he asked himself. Two were, he knew for sure. More? Maybe. He stepped swiftly inside the barn and made out the three men who were standing near a stall.

All three turned toward him.

"What's going on here, gents?" he asked pleasantly.

"Leather that gun!" Rumson barked, gesturing angrily. "This is none of your affair."

"I told you to ride out," the man beside Rumson snarled.

"I did that. But I came back when I heard the commotion. Figured somebody might need my help."

"Nobody needs your help," Rumson retorted. "Certainly not this Injun."

"What Indian?" Cimarron asked because he saw none.

Rumson pointed to the stall and Cimarron shifted position so that he was able to see inside it.

Rumson smiled and said, "We're just teaching him a little lesson, that's all. He came skulking around here begging for beef."

The man beside Rumson grinned and said, "But we decided to give him something else to eat."

Cimarron stared at War Pony who was on his knees.

The third man of the trio, who was standing just outside the stall, was gripping him by the neck and forcing his head down toward the droppings a horse had left in the stall.

"He's an ungrateful sonofabitch though," Rumson remarked. "Carey there—" he indicated the man who had first come out of the barn earlier "had to hit him with his gun butt a couple of times to try to teach him table manners. Like I said, Cimarron. You can leather that gun of yours. Unless you want to make trouble over nothing more important than that there Injun who likes to kick white men."

Cimarron hesitated a moment and then plunged his .44 into its holster. He smiled and hooked his thumbs in his cartridge belt. "Maybe that Injun's not really hungry," he commented.

"Maybe not," Rumson mused. "Simmons," he said to the man who was still gripping War Pony's neck with one hand while brandishing his six-gun with the other.

"Boss?"

"Simmons, maybe you could do something to stimulate that Injun's appetite some."

Simmons grinned and suddenly kicked War Pony, sending him sprawling face down in the droppings.

"Nothing but a nuisance, these redskins," Cimarron remarked offhandedly.

War Pony got up on his hands and knees. As he turned and saw Cimarron, Cimarron gave him a warning glance.

Simmons, aiming his six-gun at War Pony, said, "It's dinner time. Now, I already told you that twice. You going to eat that shit or am I going to put a second hole in that red ass of yours?"

Cimarron, as Simmons forced War Pony's head lower, stepped swiftly forward and pulled Carey's gun from its holster. He gave the man a shove which sent him flying toward Simmons and, when Carey collided with Simmons, he yelled, "War Pony! Up and at them!"

War Pony leaped to his feet. He brought one knee up and slammed it into Simmons' midsection just before the man fell, with Carey landing on top of him.

Cimarron tossed Carey's gun to War Pony, who trained it on the two men lying at his feet.

"Hold on there!" Rumson spluttered, and started toward Cimarron, who turned toward him and cocked his revolver, which caused Rumson to halt his advance.

"What the hell—" Rumson began, but Cimarron interrupted him.

"That man's a friend of mine."

"What man?" Rumson asked, obviously puzzled. "You know Carey? Simmons?"

"You've got yourself a muddled mind, Rumson. To you, War Pony isn't even a man, is he?"

"The Injun? He's just—"

"Shut up, goddammit!" Cimarron shouted in disgust at Rumson. "War Pony, you all right?"

War Pony nodded, his eyes on Carey and Simmons, who still cowered on the floor of the barn under the gun in his hand.

"Listen here, Cimarron," Rumson said, "we don't want trouble."

"Nor do I."

"You say this Injun's a friend of yours. Well, why don't you and him just ride on out of here and let us be?" Rumson's eyes dropped to the gun in Cimarron's hand

"We're going to do that very thing "

"Now, that's sensible. There's no need for any shooting. We were just funning that redskin only it seems he couldn't take a joke. He kicked Simmons in the ass so I admit we manhandled him a bit, but there's no harm done."

"Where's your mount?" Cimarron asked War Pony who jerked a thumb over his shoulder toward the stalls that were partially hidden in the dim interior of the barn.

"I'll get him for you," Rumson volunteered.

But, as he turned and started into the gloom, Cimarron called out, "Hold it right there, Rumson, and turn around."

When Rumson had done so, Cimarron said, "War Pony, you say, came here for beef. I say he's going to take some of your beef—him and me, we are—back to the Cheyenne-Arapaho reservation to help feed those folks down there."

"You've got no right!" Rumson bellowed.

"I've got all the right in the world," Cimarron countered. He pulled his badge from his pocket and showed it to Rumson and, as the man stared at it, apparently fascinated by it, he added, "We'll take some of your stock—how many head are you running?"

"Over a thousand," Rumson answered, "but—"

"We'll take a hundred and call it a tithing." Cimarron grinned as an agonized expression appeared on Rumson's face. "I'm just joking, Rumson. You'll be paid for the cattle we take by Agent Tracy down on the reservation. I'll guarantee payment."

"I sold cattle once to Tracy," Rumson declared angrily. "That was over two months ago and I'm still waiting for the government to pay me! I vowed I'd never sell Tracy even one more steer."

"Well," Cimarron said, "you've just broken your vow and made your second sale to Tracy through his authorized representative—namely me."

"We'll come gunning for you if you take any of Mr. Rumson's stock," Carey barked, but said no more after War Pony kicked him in the shin.

"That's a promise," Rumson said softly, his eyes on Cimarron.

"Well, War Pony and me'll just have to see that we get ourselves a good head start in that case." Cimarron, keeping his .44 trained on Rumson, edged over to where War Pony stood. He took Carey's gun from War Pony and gave him curt instructions, after which he backed up so that he could cover both Rumson and the two men who still sat on the floor.

He was silent as War Pony took the coiled rope down from the nail on which it had been hanging. But then, as War Pony went to work first on Carey and then on Simmons, he spoke to Rumson.

"I have a notion to arrest you for trespassing on Indian Territory. You are, you know."

"I'm not!" Rumson argued. "I've got a permit to be here and to graze my cattle here from the office of the Cherokee treasurer up in Caldwell, Kansas. I can show it to you!"

"Don't want to see it. Rumson, I could take you back to Fort Smith and put you in the not-very-pretty jail there while you tried to arrange to get somebody to come back here for this permit you say you have and bring it back and show it to Judge Parker and—well, by that time your ranch here'd be likely to have gone to hell on an express train. I just mention all this to make you and your boys think twice about coming gunning for War Pony and me once we head out with those hundred head of your cattle I mentioned before."

Rumson muttered an oath.

Neither he nor Cimarron spoke again as War Pony finished stringing Carey and Simmons up by the heels by means of lengths of rope thrown over the barn's rafters and tied to uprights.

Their protests went unheeded by both Cimarron and War Pony, who exchanged glances but no words as the two men hung and slowly spun, their heads almost touching the horse droppings that littered the floor of the stall.

"Him too?" War Pony asked Cimarron, pointing to Rumson.

"Him too."

"No!" Rumson cried, but then War Pony seized him and, despite his struggles, he was soon hanging upside down beside Carey and Simmons.

"We'll die like this!" Rumson, his face reddening, yelled.

"You won't," Cimarron contradicted. "That's why War Pony left all of you with your hands free. You ought to be able to untie yourselves with a little exertion. That'll occupy you in a better cause than that of tormenting an unarmed Indian."

"A voucher!" Rumson yelled. "You didn't give me a voucher for my cattle you're intending to take."

"You don't need a voucher," Cimarron called back over his shoulder, dropping Carey's gun on the floor safely out of reach of the dangling man's hands. "You got my word," he told Rumson as War Pony retrieved his mount and both men left the barn.

Once outside the barn and mounted, Cimarron and War Pony rode to where they could see Rumson's cattle grazing in the distance, the animals so thickly bunched that they hid the ground from sight.

When they reached them, Cimarron said, "Let's hit the south end of the herd down there where it snakes out some. Cut out only heavy beeves. We might as well get the Agency's money's worth while we're at it."

He spurred his black and rode toward the herd, the steers nearest him wheeling as he neared them which was what he wanted. He rode in among them and split the thick column in two and then, as War Pony passed him, he turned to the left and, yelling at the top of his voice, drove the cattle south.

War Pony, after taking up a position on the opposite side of the animals that had been cut off from the main herd, matched Cimarron's shouting.

Cimarron, slowing the black, began counting. When he had finished, he turned the pony and sent it in at a right angle toward the last of the cattle. He cut out more than a dozen of the animals, turned them and sent them thundering back toward the main body of the herd.

He held up a hand, gestured, and War Pony slowed the pony he was riding and the cattle gradually slowed their flight and finally stopped altogether to toss their heads from side to side and then begin to graze lazily again. He rode up to War Pony and pointed to the gather they had made. "There's a hundred there. Some of them are so scrawny though that if they were men they wouldn't have the strength to spit. See that one? Those two over there? Let's weed 'em out and replace them with steers that's got more meat on their bones."

It didn't take long to cut out the less weighty animals and replace them with fatter cattle from the main herd and then, when the task was completed, Cimarron and War Pony took up positions at the rear of their small herd and, flanking it, moved it out.

The sun had set by the time they reached the Darlington Agency and the sky just above the horizon was thick with clouds that were being gilded by the invisible sun. When they had the hundred head penned in the agency corral, the gilt clouds had become a purple mass and shadows were disappearing as the day's light continued to fade.

"War Pony," Cimarron said, as both men stood leaning on the poles of the corral, "did you happen to see any white men roaming about when you were on your way up to Rumson's?"

War Pony shook his head. "Maybe Nine Fingers saw some. Maybe other Elk Soldiers saw some."

"They were up north with you?"

"They go to other ranches. I go to Rumson's." War Pony looked off into the distance. "Maybe they have trouble too."

Cimarron surreptitiously studied War Pony's face. "There's no need for you to feel bad about what happened at Rumson's. You were unarmed. There were three of them to your one."

"They shamed me."

"Are you put out because they shamed you or because I saw what they were trying to do to you?"

"You know I am Elk Soldier. You know I beg white men for beef."

Cimarron reached out and put a hand on War Pony's shoulder. "A man does what he has to do the best way he knows how to do it."

War Pony brushed his hand away. "Elk Soldiers brave. Good hunters. Strong men. This Elk Soldier begs food from white men who make him a fool." He turned and leaped onto the bare back of his pony and picked up the rope rein that was looped around the animal's lower jaw.

"Where you headed?" Cimarron asked him, aware that War Pony was avoiding looking him in the eye.

"Back to camp. Cheyennes hold sacred arrows ceremony."

"What's that?"

"Medicine to bring back the power of the sacred arrows so that our people will be well. Soldiers control camp during ceremony. Crazy Dogs one day. Red Shields next day. Bow Strings next day. Elk Soldiers tomorrow on last day. I go now."

Cimarron stood watching as War Pony rode south and then

he boarded the black and rode to Tracy's residence, where he dismounted and called the agent's name.

When Tracy appeared in the doorway of his house, Cimarron said, "Brought you a hundred head of cattle. They're in your corral. I promised a Mr. Rumson you'd pay him and I hope you'll do it as prompt as you can on account of he claims he's still not been paid for stock he sold you more'n two months back."

"That's wonderful, Cimarron!" Tracy exclaimed, hurrying down the steps to shake Cimarron's hand. "Yes, yes, of course I'll see to it that he's paid promptly. In fact, I have money enough in the treasury right now to pay him directly instead of asking for an appropriation from the Bureau."

"You'll give him a good price, will you? You need beef and men like Rumson've got beef. Being stingy's no way to court cattlemen you're looking to for the meat you need."

"Of course, of course. I'll see to the matter this very minute!" Tracy started back inside his house, but then suddenly turned back to Cimarron. "Those horse thieves—were they convicted?"

Cimarron shook his head and, when Tracy's jaw dropped, he explained what had happened to the case against Farley and the others in Dodge City.

Tracy groaned and then, his shoulders slumping, disappeared inside his house.

Cimarron was about to head for the river that was not far away when he heard a woman shriek in the distance. He looked to his right and saw a man and woman battling in the middle of the dirt street in front of Drake's Trading House.

The woman shrieked a second time and swung her right arm, catching the man who was trying to defend himself from her on the shoulder.

Cimarron recognized Loretta Croft but not the man she was attacking. As he came closer to the pair, the man gave Loretta a shove that sent her careening away from him, her arms flailing wildly.

"I'll damn well do as I damn well please!" he shouted at her.

"I'll kill you, Bob Drake!" Loretta screamed and lunged. "I'll kill both of you! You and that damned Indian bitch of yours!"

As she began to scratch and bite Drake, he shoved her

away again with little effort and then, grinning, savagely backhanded her.

She went down in the dirt as Cimarron drew rein a few steps away fom her.

"You're Drake, I take it," he said to the man, who was still grinning as he stared down at the furious Loretta.

"I am," he answered without looking up at Cimarron. "If you're interested in trading, I'm the man you want to talk to."

Loretta, on her hands and knees now, scrambled toward Drake, and seized his leg with both hands. Her teeth clamped on his thigh.

"*Owwww!*" he yelled, and grabbed a handful of her hair in an attempt to break free.

Loretta held on with both of her hands and her teeth.

Drake was about to backhand her again when Cimarron slid out of the saddle and grabbed his wrist. "*Loretta, let go!*" he commanded, and shook her shoulder. When she released Drake, he shoved her out of the way. To Drake, he said, "I don't like to mind other people's business for them but neither do I take kindly to a man beating up a woman."

"Self-defense!" Drake bellowed, trying to free himself from Cimarron without succeeding. "You saw the bitch— what she did to me. A man has a right to fight for his life."

Loretta, leaping to her feet, lunged at Drake.

Cimarron put out his free hand and his flattened palm caught Loretta between her breasts, halting her. "Drake, you go back inside your place and I'll see if I can't settle Loretta down some."

"You know Loretta? Who are you?"

"Sir Galahad!" Loretta screeched. "He's come to rescue a damsel in distress—me!"

"I'm called Cimarron. Now, Drake, I'm going to let you go and if you know what's good for you, you'll git."

When Cimarron released Drake's wrist, Drake huffed, puffed, muttered something unintelligible, and then turned and stalked away.

"Now, then, Loretta, you've calmed down a bit, have you?"

"No!" she shrieked and tried to move past Cimarron.

But he caught her arm and pulled her close to him. "You go stampeding in there and that gentlemen friend of yours is

122

not likely to act altogether gentlemanly I'd say, judging by what I just saw him do to you."

"The bastard!" Loretta muttered. "I'll kill him, I swear I will. Let me go!"

"What'd he do—or what'd you do—to start all this fussing and feuding?"

"I—he—" Loretta threw back her head and howled wordlessly.

As the shrill sound pierced his ears, Cimarron winced.

When Loretta's howling subsided, he repeated his question.

Instead of answering it, she dissolved into tears that were accompanied by wrenching sobs that shook her entire body. When Cimarron released his hold on her wrist, she covered her face with her hands.

He tried to think of something to say. He couldn't. He considered withdrawing, vaguely wishing he had not interfered in this matter in the first place.

"Bob always said he loved me," Loretta wailed, her words partially muffled by her hands which still covered her face. "I gave him the best years of my life!" Her hands fell to her sides and she stared tearfully and angrily at the open door of the Trading House. "But I've got a few good years left and I'm not going to share them with him. He can have his little whore. He'll not have me!" She turned and started marching down the street toward the river.

"Where you going?" Cimarron called after her, uneasy about what she might be intending to do.

Loretta halted and stood without moving, her back to him. Then, a brief wail of words, mournful, disconsolate, "I don't *know!*"

Cimarron went up to her and put an arm meant to be comforting around her shoulders. "He threw you over for another woman, is that it?"

"Yes," she hissed, her anger surfacing once more. "He threw me over all right. But not for another woman."

"I don't follow you."

She turned and, burying her face against Cimarron's chest, wept.

He gingerly put his arms around her, aware of people watching him from the windows of the buildings lining the street.

"A child," Loretta mumbled, straightening and staring up at Cimarron. "A mere child!"

"Beg pardon?"

"*Her!*" Loretta screamed and pointed to the Trading House.

Cimarron turned his head and saw Antelope standing forlornly in the doorway. "What the hell is Antelope doing in there?"

"That's what I've been trying to tell you, dammit! Her father traded her to Bob for whiskey."

Cimarron, shaking his head, swore.

"Walks with Wolves," Loretta declared, "would sell his soul for whiskey." She sniffed. "I found Bob in bed with her—in our bed! He was grunting and snuffling on top of her like a hog rooting around in a turnip patch. I'll kill him! I'll kill both of them!"

"Calm down, honey. Why don't you go back in there and try making it up with Drake?"

"No! I never want to see him again!"

"Well, I've got to be leaving you now. I hope things work out for the two of you." For the three of you, he thought, with mixed feelings of fury and sadness.

As he started back toward his black, Loretta began to wail again.

And then she was suddenly beside him again, her face flushed, her eyes still brimming with tears. "Take me with you. I don't care where. I have no place else to go. Take me with you. *Please!*"

Cimarron looked down at the ground. He looked up at the sky. He sighed.

"Cimarron?"

"I've got me a lodge at Big Eagle's camp. You're welcome to use it until you can pull yourself together."

"Oh, thank you, Cimarron!" Loretta cried, throwing her arms around his neck.

He was taken by surprise when she kissed him fervently on the lips and he was taken by surprise again when both of them were aboard the black and Loretta, as they passed Drake's Trading House, yelled at the top of her voice, "I hope you roast in hell, Bob Drake! I truly do."

Cimarron made no comment and they rode on in silence, fording the river, and moving south toward Big Eagle's camp. When he caught sight of the troopers in the distance, he broke his silence.

"Now, what are they doing here?" he asked himself aloud.

"They're patrolling the reservation," Loretta replied, as if the question had been addressed to her.

"I kind of figured that's what they were doing. But what I wonder is why."

"There are rumors that the Northern Cheyennes are planning to leave the reservation and return north."

"To the Red Cloud Agency?"

"No. Just north. I can't say I blame them. A person has a right to live his life in the way he wants to live it without anybody giving him orders all the time or trying to make him into something he isn't. Bob Drake gave me more orders than come into any thriving mercantile company in an entire month. Do this. Do that. I'm well rid of him!"

Cimarron thought he heard Loretta sniff but he wasn't sure. Were her tears about to begin again? He hoped not. Crying women had about as much appeal to him as a scalping knife in the hands of a hostile.

When they finally reached Big Eagle's camp, he was surprised to find it apparently deserted. A quiet that seemed almost ominous hung over the lodges. But then he saw War Pony and several other Elk Soldiers appear from behind one of the lodges, some of them carrying clubs, others willow whips.

When War Pony saw him, he hurried up to him and said, "Get your woman inside your lodge. No women can be out here now. Not until sacred arrow ceremony ends."

"You got some newcomers to the camp, looks like," Cimarron observed, pointing to the two new lodges which had not been in the camp when he had left it.

"Sweet Medicine's lodge," War Pony said, pointing to the nearer of the two. "Sacred arrow lodge," he said, pointing to the other one.

"What's that singing all about?" Cimarron asked as the resonant sounds of male voices drifted in the air.

"Men sing Wolf Pup songs in Sweet Medicine's lodge. Spirit Lodge songs." He gestured abruptly, first at Loretta and then at Cimarron's lodge.

Cimarron rode up to it, dismounted, and then helped Loretta down. He lifted the flap and she entered his lodge with him close behind her.

"There's some dried buffalo jerky in that parfleche over there," he told her. "Help yourself."

"Where are you going?"

"To talk to War Pony." He ducked under the lodge flap and made his way back to where War Pony and Nine Fingers were continuing their patrol of the camp. Other pairs of Elk Soldiers were also on patrol, he noticed.

"War Pony, I saw some troopers patrolling the reservation." When War Pony made no comment, he continued, "I heard rumors that you Northern Cheyennes are planning to jump the reservation."

"Words on the wind," War Pony muttered. "Only fools and women in love listen to them."

"The rumors then, they're not true? Is that what you're saying?"

"I know you are not a woman," War Pony said stonily. "I hope you are not a fool."

Nine Fingers grunted.

War Pony said, "Ceremony nearly over. We go now to Sweet Medicine's lodge."

"Mind if I come along?" Cimarron asked. "I'd like to see what's going on in there if that won't offend anybody."

War Pony gave him an appraising glance and then nodded.

Cimarron began to follow him, but they suddenly found their way blocked by Walks with Wolves, who had emerged from his lodge waving a nearly empty whiskey bottle in his hand. As Walks with Wolves began to sing a song that was a mixture of Cheyenne and English words, War Pony, without a word, raised the willow whip in his hand and brought it down on Walks with Wolves' shoulders.

Walks with Wolves bellowed his pain, cringing as War Pony's whip struck him again and again.

War Pony seized the bottle from his hand and smashed it against one of the stones circling a fire pit. He continued whipping Walks with Wolves, who, with his hands raised to protect his face, stumbled backward whimpering and finally managed to crawl back inside his lodge.

"Camp must be quiet for sacred arrows ceremony," War Pony said bluntly.

At that moment, a dog came bounding out from between two lodges and began to bark.

War Pony reached down, seized the dog by one hind leg, swung it up over his head, and then brought it down, smashing its skull against the fire pit's stones. "We go now," he said to Cimarron, dropping the dead dog.

As Cimarron followed him into the dark lodge, the singing grew louder and he was able to make out a number of men seated cross-legged on the ground, all of them joining in the song.

"Spirit Lodge," War Pony said, pointing to the tall rectangular shape towering above the floor which was covered with a white cloth and bound with rawhide thongs.

Cimarron noted the packed and painted pipe, its bowl resting against the earth, its stem leaning against one of the horns of a buffalo skull. He watched a man rise and pick up the pipe and place it beneath the covered Spirit Lodge.

"Red Berry gives pipe to the Maiyun inside Spirit Lodge," War Pony said in a low voice.

Cimarron glanced at the four sacred arrows that leaned against a thin branch that was set in the upright forks of two other branches, which had been implanted in the ground. Two flint arrow points were aimed at the sky. Two touched the ground.

"The Mahuts," War Pony whispered, pointing to the sacred arrows.

One of the men seated near the arrows held out his hands, palms up. The man next to him spat into them.

"Sky Gets Dark spits sacred sweet root," War Pony said.

Sky Gets Dark rose and picked up the four sacred arrows, carefully wrapping their points in buffalo membranes. He placed them in a kit fox-skin quiver and, with the help of the man into whose palms he had spat the sacred sweet root, he rolled the quiver inside a buffalo hide outer cover.

He rose, the quiver cradled in his arms.

"It ends," War Pony told Cimarron. "Now the world is made new for us again."

Sky Gets Dark made his way out of the lodge, the other men, Cimarron and War Pony among them, following him, and walked toward the sacred arrow lodge chanting, "Piveh, piveh!"

"Ha Ho!" War Pony shouted, and the other men joined their voices to his.

"Ha ho, ha ho!"

"What'd Sky Gets Dark say?" Cimarron asked. "What are all you fellows saying?"

"Sky Gets Dark says 'Good, good!' " War Pony replied. "We say 'Thank you, thank you!' "

"Who's this Sweet Medicine you mentioned?"

"Cheyenne. Lived long time back. Taught us what he learned from Mahuts on Sacred Mountain. Now we Cheyennes are strong again because of sacred arrows. Now we will be free to live as Sweet Medicine taught us we must live"

Cimarron glanced at War Pony, saw the broad smile on his face, and thought of the rumor Loretta had told him about the possibility of the Cheyennes leaving the reservation.

"Piveh! Piveh!"

"Ha ho! Ha ho!"

As the chanting of the Cheyennes around him continued, he thought of the troopers he had seen patrolling the reservation on his way back to Big Eagle's camp, and a frown appeared on his face.

9

Cimarron returned to his lodge to find Loretta standing outside it. She followed him into it and watched as he picked up his parfleche, which still contained some buffalo jerky, and then a blanket.

"Where are you going?" she asked him. "Aren't you sleeping here tonight?"

"Nope." He went back outside, followed by Loretta and, as he was about to mount his pony, she said, "I hope I'm not in your way."

"I find having a pretty woman like yourself in my way's about as welcome as walking through the world with the wind at my back." He gave her a grin and then, "I'm expecting some horse thieves to come rustling the pony herd sometime and I plan on being there to meet them if they come tonight. I'll be sleeping out though I won't be liking it considering you're back here in my lodge maybe getting lonesome for some company."

Loretta smiled. "If the horse thieves you mentioned—If they don't show up—"

"I'll be back about dawn."

Loretta stood staring after Cimarron as he rode away from the lodge toward the spot where the camp's pony herd was grazing.

When he reached it, he was surprised to find that the herd seemed to have doubled in size. He was sure there were at least twice as many animals in it now as there had been before. Maybe more.

As the boys assigned to guard the mounts stared curiously at him, he got out of the saddle and, after leaning the barrel of his rifle against the trunk of an aspen, sat down on the ground and braced his back against the tree's trunk, his forearms resting on his bent knees. He pushed his hat back on his head and looked around.

To his left the land was bare of any growth except for occasional patches of bunch grass. To his right and some distance away was a thick stand of pin oaks. Ahead of him a low hill rose.

As the first stars appeared in the sky above him, he opened his parfleche, took out a thin strip of jerky, and began to chew it.

He was aware of the eyes of the boys upon him but he gave no sign of that fact. They're more interested in scouting me than they are in keeping their eyes on the animals they've been set to look after, he thought with faint annoyance as he ate a second piece of jerky.

Time passed and the boys lost interest in him. As more stars appeared in the sky and the moon began to rise, they took up positions in a rough circle around the herd.

Cimarron, his eyes on the trees that swayed faintly in the soft breeze that had begun to blow, snapped alert when he heard the rustle of something even softer than the breeze. He drew his .44 but his body remained motionless as he listened intently.

Behind him. That's where the sound had come from. The boys didn't seem to have heard it. As the sound grew louder, he was on his feet and turning, his thumb drawing back the hammer of his Colt.

"Cimarron!"

"Loretta." He holstered his gun. "What are you doing out here?"

"You were right. I was lonesome."

"Well, go on back to the lodge and be lonesome back there. I don't want you mixed up in any trouble that might start out here tonight."

Loretta sat down at the base of the tree. "It's such a nice night, isn't it?" When she received no response, she said, "I suppose I should have told someone long before this."

"Told somebody what?"

"About Bob. About Bob Drake and Enoch Tracy."

"You trying to tease me? Or do you want me to keep on trying to pry loose what you're so eager to say anyway?"

"They're crooks, both of them."

Cimarron leaned his rifle against the tree and sat down beside Loretta. "They steal part of the annuities that are meant for the Indians," he remarked casually.

Loretta turned toward him, moonlight bathing her face. "Now, how did you know that?"

"When I was in Drake's place that time I saw the letters U.S. stenciled on that sack you were hauling out from the storeroom. Planned on looking into that little matter first chance I got."

"You could arrest Bob, couldn't you? I mean he is a thief as I've told you. You could put him in prison, couldn't you?"

"You'd like that?"

"Oh, would I ever! You will arrest him then?"

"And you'd testify against him?"

"With the utmost pleasure, yes."

"You could get proof about what Drake's doing?"

"Tracy too. Yes, I could. Bob keeps two sets of books. I know where he keeps the ones that reveal his thieving."

"I didn't figure Tracy'd be in on a scheme like you're talking about."

"Well, he is. You can take my word for it. Both of them are in it up to their eyeballs."

"I remember hearing that the Indians didn't get any corn or flour in the last annuity shipment."

"Now you know why they didn't. Because Tracy held it back. He gave it to Drake who then sold it to the Cheyennes and Arapahos—those of them who could pay for it, that is. They exploit the Indians in every way they can. They have some of the women tanning buffalo robes for them—for a mere pittance. Bob gives them tokens instead of cash money to trade for goods at his place but the Indians aren't ever told exactly how much they're worth. The truth is they're worth whatever Bob decides they're worth at any given time. It's scandalous. It's a frightful way to behave."

"You've known about these shenanigans for how long?"

"Well—" Loretta looked down. She smoothed her skirt. "Well, for a while." She looked up at Cimarron again. "I was a woman in love, Cimarron. Please try to understand."

"Oh, I understand all right. Now you're not a woman in love and you want me to punish the man you loved for you."

"No, it's not that way at all. It really isn't." She gave

Cimarron an appealing glance, one that he thought might also be promising, before adding, "I just think it's high time I did the right thing. For those poor Indians, I mean."

"Uh-huh."

Loretta, as she leaned toward Cimarron, let her hand come to rest on his thigh. "I'm really very much happier when I do the right thing. I haven't been happy for such a long time and then when Walks with Wolves sold that child to Bob—I think being here with you is the right thing for me. You're a rather attractive man, Cimarron."

His hand rose and his fingers slid along the scar on his face.

"Oh, that!" Loretta said with a wave of her hand. "That scar makes you—more interesting. It doesn't make your eyes less—" she searched for a word and came up with, "disturbing. In a truly thrilling way though. Your lips—" She placed hers on them.

Cimarron savored her kiss for a moment before drawing away from her and remarking, "I'm another way you want to punish Bob Drake."

"Beg pardon?"

"If you and me—and if he found out about it—why, I reckon it wouldn't make him too happy."

"He doesn't care a hoot in hell about me! Not anymore, he doesn't."

"Don't you go and be too sure about that, honey. I've known men in my time who'd black a woman's eyes one minute and then come crawling to her the next begging for a kind word—for starters."

"You think Bob might still—" Loretta seized Cimarron and kissed him again. "But I don't want Bob Drake. I do want you. I want you to take me. Do with me what you will. That time when you came into the Trading House, I felt weak just watching you—the way you moved, the way your eyes looked right through me and saw every innermost secret I ever cherished."

Why the hell not, Cimarron thought. Loretta was here and he was here and Bob Drake was not, so . . . He put his arms around her and drew her close to him. He kissed her gently at first and then more firmly, causing her to moan.

She suddenly pushed him away from her. "Those trees over there. We could go there. No one could see us there." She sprang to her feet, grabbed his hand and, when he was also on his feet, led him quickly toward and then into the shelter of the trees.

Loretta was panting once they were under the trees, whether with lust or exertion, Cimarron wasn't certain.

"I forgot to bring my blanket," he told her.

"We won't need a blanket," she assured him. "We have each other."

Cimarron wondered what the connection was as she sat down on the ground, lay back, and raised her arms invitingly to him.

He knelt down, lifted her dress, and spread her legs, surprised to find that she was wearing no undergarments. Her naked flesh was warm to his touch and her hands that were resting lightly on his loins stirred him. He unstrapped his cartridge belt, dropped it on the ground, and then unbuttoned his jeans, which he shoved down below his knees.

He lay down upon her, not yet hard, and adjusted his body so that his legs were between hers. He nuzzled the base of her throat as his hands slid beneath her buttocks and lifted her slightly.

"Where is it?" Loretta murmured.

"Right where it belongs only it's not ready yet, honey."

"I want it."

"You'll get it, I promise. Just give me a minute." He rubbed himself against her and, as he did so, he began to stiffen. "There it goes." He began to probe her in a deliberately tantalizing fashion, a technique he found as provocative for himself as it was for most women.

When he felt her becoming moist, he probed more deeply— deftly and with an erotic precision.

Loretta thrust herself against him eagerly and he let himself slide all the way into her. But then he quickly withdrew again—but not all the way.

"Don't!" she cried.

He plunged all the way into her and she moaned and her arms seized him, her fingernails biting into his back.

He moved slowly up and down, up and down, and then, as Loretta wrapped her legs around his thighs, he twisted his pelvis, first to the right, then to the left.

Loretta twisted too. When Cimarron moved to the right,

she moved to the left. When he moved to the left, she moved to the right.

"Tell me when," she whispered in his ear.

He felt her hands slide down his spine and come to rest on his bare buttocks.

"Now?" she asked, her tongue teasing his earlobe.

"Soon," he promised, and kept at it. Then, less than a minute later, he grunted, "*Now!*"

Just before he ejaculated, Loretta thrust a finger into him and, when he did flood her, his mind reeled and his body blazed with pure pleasure as she continued probing him.

He shuddered.

So did Loretta. She withdrew her finger and they clung to each other, Cimarron throbbing hotly within her, her body quivering beneath him as she kept repeating, "Oh. Oh. *Oh!*"

A giggle.

Cimarron raised himself up and looked at her. "What's funny?"

"What?"

"You giggled."

"I didn't."

"I heard you."

The giggle again.

Cimarron pulled out of her and, kneeling, squinted into the surrounding darkness

A voice called out something in Cheyenne and at the same time he was able to make out the crouching figures of several boys watching him and Loretta from the undergrowth beneath the trees.

"Git!" he yelled at them, and was greeted with several shrill giggles. He went almost instantly limp.

"Who is it?" Loretta asked, sitting up and pulling down her skirt.

"A bunch of peeping Toms," Cimarron replied, rising and pulling up his jeans. "*Git!*" he yelled again, and shook a fist at the boys, none of whom had moved. He buttoned his jeans, found a stone, and threw it at them.

The boys ducked.

"Show's over!" he shouted. "You boys don't git, I'm going to cut yours off so's you'll never get to practice the act you just saw us performing!"

"How dare they spy on us like that?" Loretta blustered.

"Easy. Kids got more curiosity about what we were just doing than a barfly's got calluses on his elbows." As Cimarron took several steps toward the boys, they scattered and soon disappeared. "Watching us was a whole lot more fun for them, I reckon, than minding the pony herd."

He picked up his cartridge belt and was strapping it low on his hips when he heard a yell that was quickly followed by another.

"Those boys are still mocking us," Loretta declared fretfully as she got to her feet.

No, Cimarron thought, listening. That's not why they're yelping. Something's happening. "You stay here in the trees," he told Loretta, and began to run through the darkness, almost tripping over a deadfall as he sprinted toward the sound of the boys' voices, which were still piercing the night.

As he came out of the shelter of the trees, he saw the three riders circling the herd as the boys scattered, yipping their alarm, in all directions to escape the frightened ponies that were wildly milling about.

Without slowing his pace, he veered to the right and headed for his black. He was halfway to it when several ponies suddenly wheeled and cut him off from the animal. He halted a moment and then ran to the right, rounding the last of the fleeing ponies, his eyes on the rifle in its boot behind his saddle.

When he reached the black, he leaped into the saddle, gave the reins a tug, and sent the black back the way he had just come, dodging a stray pony that galloped past him as he went, heading straight for Farley, who was slashing at the herd with a coiled rope to turn them north.

Suddenly, one of the other two riders cut in front of Cimarron, forcing him to draw rein to avoid a collision. In that brief time, Farley turned, spotted him, and pulled a six-gun from his holster.

Cimarron dropped down against the neck of his black, drew his own revolver, and came up fast on Farley.

"You shoot, Farley, our cartridges'll kiss on their way past each other. You might kill my pony but I'll kill you."

Farley hesitated a moment, but then, as dust swirled up around him, he swiftly turned his horse and headed away from Cimarron, who set out in pursuit of his quarry.

He was aware of hooves pounding the ground off to his

right and behind him, but he kept his eyes on Farley, not wanting to lose sight of the man for a moment. As the hoofbeats grew louder, he spurred his black and the animal picked up speed.

But the black wasn't fast enough and Cimarron swore vehemently as the ponies leading the herd galloped between him and Farley. He was forced to halt as the rest of the herd streamed past him in what seemed to him to be an endless procession of flying feet and manes.

A shot sounded and he heard it ping past him. He turned his head and saw one of the two men who were running the herd riding toward him on its western flank, a carbine in his hands.

Cimarron leaped to the ground, positioned himself behind the black's rump, and then, as the rider with the carbine came closer to him, he fired at the man.

Missed him, he thought angrily, and incorrectly. The dust those ponies are kicking up's enough to choke a man to death and blind him into the bargain. He took aim again as the rider came still closer to him, easing back the hammer of his Colt, but he didn't fire because suddenly the man swayed, dropped his carbine, and fell from the saddle.

Cimarron didn't give him a second glance as he quickly climbed back into the saddle and set out after Farley again, the ponies galloping in the same direction. As he came up on their eastern flank, he spotted the rider just ahead of him. More trouble, he thought.

The rider looked back over his shoulder, let out a yell, and then fired at Cimarron, who returned the fire, missing his target the first time but hitting the man with his second shot.

The rider galloped on but he was obviously having trouble staying in the saddle.

Cimarron spurred the black and, when he caught up with the rider he had wounded, he pulled his left boot from its stirrup and struck out with it, kicking the man in the ribs and sending him sprawling to the ground between his horse and the galloping herd.

As he rode on after Farley, who had far outdistanced the herd, he heard the man behind him scream in agony. He looked back and saw several ponies trample the man and then gallop on, leaving behind them a crushed hulk that no longer moved or looked even vaguely human.

Even odds now, Cimarron thought grimly and rode on, his eyes on Farley.

Farely, when he saw Cimarron behind him, spurred his mount, turned, and got off a snap shot that went over Cimarron's head.

Cimarron shortened the distance between himself and Farley. When he was almost up to the man and Farley was about to fire at him again, he holstered his .44 and ripped his Winchester from its boot. He swung it up and then brought it down.

Farley screamed as the barrel of the rifle stuck his wrist, knocking his six-gun from his hand. But he didn't slow his pace and Cimarron, determined now to get his man, raked his spurs along the black's flanks.

The animal responded with an abrupt burst of speed, and, as it did, Cimarron booted his rifle and threw his right leg over the black's neck. He lunged then, hurling himself at Farley. The force of his leap knocked Farley out of the saddle and both men went down, Farley hitting the ground first with Cimarron landing on top of him.

Farley gave Cimarron a shove, but Cimarron, managing to get a grip on Farley's shirt, hauled Farley up and then shoved him away.

He reached for his gun, but before his hand could touch its butt, Farley sprang forward and threw a right uppercut that slammed into Cimarron's jaw, snapping his head backward. As he staggered backward, Farley came in on him, crouching low, and delivered several body blows in quick succession.

As Farley threw another fist, Cimarron, regaining his balance and his breath, blocked it with his left forearm. At the same time he swung his right fist and landed a solid hit on Farley's jaw that he quickly followed up with a swift left-hand punch which struck the side of Farley's head.

As Farley swung again, Cimarron went in under the man's right arm and hooked both fists, one after the other, into Farley's midsection. He stepped back as Farley doubled over gasping. Breathing heavily, he disobeyed his instinct to reach for his Colt. He didn't want to shoot Farley, didn't want to kill him. He wanted to hit him and hit him hard. He wanted to hurt the man he had been hunting for so long and who had almost killed him back along the trail. If Farley wanted to fight now, well, he'd give him a good one.

"I'm just getting going," he said, his voice cold. "This knuckle and skull game of yours suits me just fine."

Farley sprang forward, his head lowered, and butted Cimarron in the midsection.

Cimarron took the blow and reacted to it by bringing his right knee up fast and hard.

When Farley sceamed, Cimarron smiled, and his smile broadened as Farley straightened, his fingers touching and then swiftly withdrawing from his nose, which Cimarron's knee had broken. He watched Farley's eyes squeeze shut as a result of the pain and he watched the blood flowing from Farley's broken nose and smashed lips.

"I'll bust your skull as easy as I just did your nose, Farley. You want to go one more round with me?"

Farley groaned. "You're a dirty damned fighter, Cimarron."

"But a fighter, you got to admit. I fight clean when I can, dirty when I have to. I do what it takes to win. Now, you and me're moving out of here."

"My horse—"

"You've seen the last of that horse. He's running with the Cheyennes' pony herd now. By the time the Indians round up those ponies again, we'll be well on our way back to Fort Smith."

"Like hell you'll be!"

At the sound of the man's voice that had come from behind him, Cimarron threw himself to the ground, rolled over, and came up with his Colt in his hand and blazing.

He got slowly to his feet as the man who had been about to shoot him in the back crumpled and went down, his six-gun falling beside his body.

"I thought I'd killed your friend back there awhile ago," he remarked to Farley. "Guess I didn't. But he sure as hell is dead now, looks like." Cimarron gestured with the barrel of his gun. "Start walking, Farley. That way."

When Farley obeyed his order, Cimarron followed him on foot until he reached his black and then he stepped into the saddle. "I'll be riding right behind you, Farley. You make a run for it, you'll find yourself running straight through the gates of hell and right on into the fire."

"That's a good gun," Farley commented as they came to the spot where his revolver lay in the grass. "Shame to let it lie there."

"Pick it up," Cimarron commanded. When Farley had done so, he said, "Hand it up here to me—butt first."

Gripping the gun's barrel, Farley did so and looked crestfallen as Cimarron shoved the weapon into his waistband.

When they reached the stand of pin oaks a few minutes later, Cimarron let out a yell. "Loretta!" He waited and, when she neither answered him nor put in an appearance, he called her name a second time. When she still did not answer or appear, he shrugged and ordered Farley to keep moving.

They had not gone far when a band of Cheyennes appeared in the distance, War Pony leading them.

"Where did they go?" War Pony asked as he reached Cimarron and drew rein, the other Cheyennes clustered around him.

Cimarron wasn't sure whether he had been asking about the ponies or the thieves. "I killed two of the jaspers back along the trail a bit. The ponies went that way," he said, pointing in the direction in which the herd had headed.

Before the Cheyennes could ride out, Cimarron pulled Farley's gun from his waistband and handed it to War Pony. "Maybe you can use that. Call it a parting gift. I'll be leaving your camp now. I've got to be taking this horse thief to Fort Smith. It's been real good knowing you, War Pony." He held out his hand and, as War Pony shook it, he said, "I hope you Cheyennes make out all right. If I'm ever back this way, I'll stop by and say hello."

"We will not meet again," War Pony said solemnly.

"Why'd you say that?" Cimarron asked, but he suspected that he knew the answer to his question.

When War Pony didn't answer it, Cimarron said, "Before you go I got something I want to ask you. Those boys you had watching your ponies, well, they contented themselves with watching me and a woman I was with earlier tonight. One of them yelled something at me." He repeated the Cheyenne words as best he could and his eyebrows rose in surprise as War Pony laughed along with the other braves who were close enough to have heard what he had said. "What do those words mean?" he asked gruffly as the laughter swirled around him.

War Pony, smiling, repeated the Cheyenne words and then translated them. "White man better than bull elk."

Cimarron frowned, puzzled. "I don't see what's so funny about that."

"Cheyennes know," War Pony declared, "that spirits live in animals. Spirit of love live in bull elk. Bull elk calls. Female elk always come. Always."

Cimarron felt his face flushing as War Pony's smile broadened and, behind him, Nine Fingers erupted again in raucous laughter.

When the Cheyennes moved out after the pony herd, Cimarron rode north thinking about Loretta and wondering where she was. *Back in my lodge*, he finally decided. *The shooting must have scared her and she took to her heels to find someplace safe.*

"Where you marching me?" Farley asked sullenly as he and Cimarron moved on through the moonless night.

"You heard what I told War Pony. I'm taking you to Fort Smith to stand trial. But before I set out for there, we're going to make a stop at Fort Reno for some provisions I plan to buy."

"You expect me to walk all the way?"

"I figure on doing some dickering with a friend of mine at Fort Reno for a cavalry mount for you."

"That's real nice of you, Cimarron," Farley sneered.

"Not nice at all. Just practical. It'd take me till judgment day to get you back to Arkansas otherwise."

Some time later, they came to Big Eagle's camp and Cimarron halted in front of his lodge. "Loretta!" he called out. When he received no reply, he dismounted and, keeping his gun trained on Farley, threw back the lodge cover and peered inside to discover that the lodge was empty. *Now where the hell*, he wondered, *is that woman. I can't go hunting her. I've got Farley to see to.* He suddenly remembered something War Pony had said about Big Eagle. *My father understands some white words.*

Marching Farley before him, he made his way to Big Eagle's lodge. He called the chief's name, and when he received a faint reply, he shoved Farley inside and went in after him to find Big Eagle lying on a buffalo robe near the low fire that was burning in the center of the lodge.

Using a mixture of words and signs, he tried to convey to the chief that he wanted War Pony, if he saw Loretta, to tell her that he had to return to Fort Smith.

When he had finished, Big Eagle nodded curtly and Cimarron, hoping the old man had gotten the message straight, ordered Farley out of the lodge. He followed him outside, mounted his black, and marched Farley north, heading for Fort Reno.

10

The notes of a bugle announcing Reveille woke Cimarron and he sat up, tossing his blanket aside, and glanced over at Farley whom he had tied to a tree before making camp the night before.

He was shaking out and pulling on his boots when the trumpeter sounded Stable Call a little later. He got up and stood staring off into the distance at Fort Reno.

"We ought to get moving," Farley muttered. "That trumpeter will be sounding Breakfast Call any minute now."

Not for an hour or more, Cimarron thought. Not until after he's sounded Recall.

"I'm hungry," Farley whined.

Me too, Cimarron thought but kept silent.

"Untie me," Farley pleaded. "My arms are as stiff as boards. You tied me too tight last night."

Cimarron watched the activities taking place in the fort without responding.

"You're a cold-blooded sonofabitch, Cimarron. You like to make a man suffer."

"But I hate hearing him complain about it. Shut up, Farley. We'll go to the fort when I say we go."

He watched as troopers, under the supervision of the officer of the day, herded the horses from the fort. When the officer had selected the day's grazing ground, posted vedettes and guards, and then started back for the fort, Cimarron untied Farley, mounted his black, and moved his prisoner out.

When they reached the fort, he rode up to the crude commandant's office. "Lieutenant Kendrick!"

When Kendrick appeared in the doorway, he said, "Got some news for you that you'll likely find interesting."

"Indeed, Cimarron?"

Cimarron pointed to Farley. "This man here's a horse thief I caught. I'm taking him back to Fort Smith to stand trial. Kendrick, would you toss him in your guardhouse temporarily so I won't have to keep one eye on him and one on you while you and me have ourselves a little talk?"

"Private Landers!" Kendrick called out and beckoned.

When the trooper he had summoned came up to him and saluted, Kendrick, said, "Take this man and put him in the guardhouse."

"Yes, sir."

As Landers started to march Farley away, the trumpeter sounded Breakfast Call.

"I'm hungry enough to starve to death!" Farley called back over his shoulder.

"Feed the prisoner, Private Landers," Kendrick ordered. Then, "Shall we go to the mess tent, Cimarron?"

"I appreciate your hospitality, Kendrick. To tell you the truth, I'm hungry enough to eat a whole horse—raw."

"Come along then."

When Cimarron and Kendrick were seated opposite one another at a plank table in the mess tent, Cimarron asked, "You know Bob Drake up at Darlington?"

"The trader? Yes, I know him by sight."

"You know Agent Tracy, of course."

"Of course."

A trooper placed plates of beef hash and some hardtack on the table and then filled two tin cups with coffee which he placed next to the plates.

Cimarron ate ravenously and, when his hash was almost gone, he stabbed his fork in Kendrick's direction and said, "Drake and Tracy are stealing part of the Indians' annuity shipments."

Kendrick almost choked on a piece of hardtack he was chewing. "Preposterous!" he spluttered. "I don't believe it."

"I happen to think it's true but I can't prove it and even if I could proving it's not my job. I've got no jurisdiction here on the reservation." He forked the last of his hash into his mouth, chewed, swallowed, drank some coffee, and said, "You do have jurisdiction, Kendrick."

"Cimarron, you can't go around making wild accusations

which are in no way substantiated by any slight shred of proof!"

"Simmer down, Kendrick." Cimarron broke a piece of hardtack and shoved half of it into his mouth and began to chew. "You ought to take yourself a look around in Drake's storeroom. I'm willing to wager you'll find some government supplies in there that Drake's been selling to the Indians. I saw one sack myself. Then there's Loretta Croft."

"I understand she and Drake are—uh—"

"They are. Or were. Thing is, she told me Drake keeps two sets of books. If you were to find the set that shows what he stole and what he did with it, you could nail him. Loretta knows where he keeps that second set of books. She told me she did."

"I suppose I can go to the Trading House and have a talk with Miss Croft."

"Maybe. Maybe not. She's not likely to be there. She and Drake had words. Something approaching a fistfight if the truth's to be told. She came to me for—uh, protection, and I stowed her away in my lodge at Big Eagle's camp but then—well, the next thing I knew she was gone "

"Where?"

"Damned if I know. But you ought to be able to find her and get her to point the finger at Drake."

"And you claim that Enoch Tracy is in collusion with Drake?"

"If collusion means crooked, that's the word for Tracy too. They're partners, him and Drake, according to Loretta."

"You believe the woman? She does not have the most savory reputation, I'm sorry to say, Cimarron "

"Who she beds and how's not the issue, Kendrick, and neither is the state of her morals, which may have tarnished her reputation some. If she can hand you those books she spoke of—what I'm getting at is you'd accept them from the hot and horny hands of old Lucifer himself, now wouldn't you?"

Kendrick nodded thoughtfully. "Those poor Indians just do not have a fair chance."

"Not in our white world that's swallowing them up and spitting them out in a shape their own parents wouldn't even recognize."

"Agents cheat them. Traders cheat them. Peddlers sell

145

them whiskey and run peyote buttons to them from down in Mexico.''

"Shameful.''

"Opiates are not the answer to their problems.''

"What are the answers to their problems, Kendrick?''

Kendrick leaned back in his chair and folded his hands on the table in front of him. "I don't know. What it all seems to boil down to is we don't know what to do with them or where to put them. We're taking a primitive people—nomadic tribes of hunters for the most part—and trying to reshape them into white Protestant farmers. It will never work.''

"You're right. It won't.''

"Lieutenant Kendrick, sir,'' said a trooper as he approached the table and then halted and saluted.

"Corporal Maguire!'' Kendrick exclaimed. "What are you doing here? You're supposed to be on patrol on the reservation.''

"Yes, sir, I am. I mean, I was. Sir, Sergeant Fowler sent me down here to report to you.''

"Well, let's have it, soldier. Report what to me?''

"Big Eagle and his people have left the reservation, sir. When we discovered the fact that he was gone—his camp was empty and all the food gone from it too—we reported to Agent Tracy, who told us he'd just had word from one of the Southern Cheyenne camps that their ponies had been stolen two days ago. All of them. Tracy believes that Big Eagle's warriors stole the ponies to use in their flight.''

"You're sure about this, soldier?''

"Sergeant Fowler is, sir. He told me to tell you that Agent Tracy telegraphed the Central Superintendency and the people there, they got in touch with General Sheridan and he sent word back to Darlington through the superintendency that the Fourth Cavalry was to pursue the Indians. We're supposed to capture as many as we can and kill the rest. General Sheridan said they could endanger the peace along the whole Kansas frontier as they head north.''

Kendrick swore and slammed a fist down on the table, rattling the tin cups.

A low whistle escaped from between Cimarron's teeth. "What are you going to do, Kendrick?'' he inquired.

"Corporal,'' Kendrick said, "have the trumpeter sound Assembly.''

"Yes, sir."

When the corporal had gone, Cimarron said, "You're going after them."

"I am. You heard the corporal. General Sheridan has given us our orders."

"To catch or kill the Cheyennes."

Kendrick nodded curtly, rose, and left the mess tent, Cimarron right behind him.

He shouted several commands and then disappeared inside the commandant's quarters. When he came out again several minutes later, he called Cimarron's name.

But Cimarron was gone.

When he came within sight of the Darlington Agency, Cimarron didn't slow the black but sent it galloping across the river. He didn't halt the animal until he was in front of Drake's Trading House.

There he dismounted and began to pound on the door when he found it locked. "Drake!" he yelled but it was not Drake who answered him.

A shrill voice called out, "Help!"

Cimarron, without a moment's hesitation, stepped back and then slammed his shoulder against the wooden door, splintering it.

Inside the building he found Antelope bound to one of the uprights that supported the roof.

"Cimarron!" she exclaimed when she recognized him.

He hurriedly untied her and then asked, "Where's Drake?"

Antelope shook her head.

"Well, it don't much matter where he is. It's you I came here for."

Antelope's eyes brightened. "You want me now?"

"Hold on, honey. That's not what I had in mind. Your people's headed north and I reckon they're on their way up to their old stamping grounds north of the Platte River. I figured you might want to catch up and go along with them."

"I will go. It is bad here."

"You're all right, are you?"

She nodded.

Cimarron thumbed cartridges from his belt and reloaded his Colt. "Let's go."

Outside, he helped Antelope into the saddle and then climbed into it himself. They rode up the wide dirt street and then around the two-story Indian school and out onto the plain again.

They continued riding for some time, neither of them speaking as Cimarron searched for sign of the Cheyennes.

He found it just east of the Antelope Hills, and he drew rein and studied the ground carefully. There was a narrow trail suggesting that the Indians were traveling in a long line rather than in a tight group. He made out the tracks left by the two poles of a travois. Big Eagle, he thought. The man must be too sick to sit a horse. He could think of no other explanation for the evidence of a travois—a single travois—since he knew that the Cheyennes had left their lodges behind and were evidently traveling light in order to make better time. They had taken food according to Corporal Maguire, and probably only such other items that were absolutely necessary to their survival. Like guns, he thought grimly.

He spurred the black and moved out, following the trail, and he caught his first glimpse of the Cheyennes up ahead of him just after the sun had passed its meridian. He galloped toward them and, when he saw several men, Nine Fingers among them, halt and turn to face him with rifles raised, he took off his hat, waved it, and shouted Nine Fingers' name.

As the rifles went down, Cimarron rode up to Nine Fingers and asked, "Where's War Pony?"

Nine Fingers turned and pointed north.

Cimarron rode along the western flank of the fleeing Cheyennes, noticing as he did so the travois on which Big Eagle was lying with his eyes closed, heading for the front of the column.

"War Pony!" he shouted and, when War Pony looked back over his shoulder, Cimarron rode up to him, and said, "I brought you this here stray."

War Pony almost smiled.

His change of expression did not escape Cimarron's notice. "Hop on down now, honey," he said to Antelope.

When Antelope had joined the women, Cimarron rode along beside War Pony a moment before remarking, "There's trouble traveling the trail behind you."

"Soldiers?"

"Some of the Fourth Cavalry. But you've got yourself a

148

head start. Still, you've got Big Eagle with you and he's going to slow you down the way he's traveling."

War Pony nodded.

"You give any thought to hiding him someplace safe with maybe a woman or two to look after him? You could send somebody back for him once you've got wherever it is you're going."

"We run from reservation now because of Big Eagle. He goes home to die."

Cimarron realized that War Pony had rejected his suggestion and he was not surprised by the reaction; he knew his suggestion had not been a very good one, but he had made it because, from the moment he had heard Corporal Maguire give General Sheridan's orders to Kendrick, he had found himself wanting to see War Pony and the other Cheyennes escape from the reservation, from the degradation reservation life imposed upon a proud people, but most of all from a world that was not theirs and would never be. Should never be, he amended thoughtfully. They've got their own ways and they're good ways, by and large.

"You come to warn us?"

War Pony's question interrupted Cimarron's thoughts.

"I did."

War Pony glanced at him.

"I think you're doing the right thing, maybe that's why, if you're wondering."

"We break law."

"White man's law."

"You are law."

"Dammit, War Pony, don't go and make things any tougher for me than they already are. I'm doing what I think's right and that's all there is to it."

War Pony turned his head and rode on, Cimarron keeping pace with him.

"War Pony, maybe you could keep an eye on Antelope. If her daddy—"

"Walks with Wolves not with us."

"He stayed on the reservation?"

"Went to Southern Cheyennes. Wants whiskey white trader Drake sells him."

"I'm real glad to hear that. Antelope's better off without him."

149

"Without Warrior Woman."

"Her too."

"I would take Antelope as wife. But she wants you."

"Well, she's not got me nor will she have me. You tell her that."

"She know good man when she see one."

"Then she ought to be smart enough to know you're a good man."

War Pony said nothing.

"I'm heading back," Cimarron announced. "Maybe I can find a way to slow down those troopers who're bent on bringing you back. Maybe I can send them off on some kind of wild goose chase. You take good care of yourself, War Pony."

He wheeled his black and galloped back along the western flank of the Cheyennes. It wasn't long before he had lost sight of them completely.

He had almost reached the Darlington Agency when he saw two riders coming toward him from the direction of the agency.

As he came closer to the two men he was surprised to find that it was Enoch Tracy and Bob Drake who were riding toward him. He was even more surprised to see that both men were now wearing six-guns. When he reached them, he nodded to them and said, "You boys out gunning for Cheyennes, are you?"

"You've spotted them?" Drake asked.

"Which way are they headed?" Tracy asked.

"Due north," Cimarron answered. "But it'll take more than the two of you to convince them to turn back. They've got rifles, some of them have, and I figure they might have them loaded although I don't know where they could've laid their hands on any ammunition seeing as how you wouldn't issue them any, Tracy."

"There's been a Kiowa trader roaming the reservation," Tracy declared. "He's been selling ammunition to any Indian with the wherewithal to buy it or trade for it."

"Cavalry's coming," Cimarron said. "Though I haven't yet laid eyes on them."

Tracy's horse snorted, pawed the earth, and moved forward a few paces until it was just beyond Cimarron.

"Loretta Croft laid eyes on you," Drake said, staring at Cimarron.

"She tagged along with me after you two had your little set-to, if that's what you're getting at."

"I saw her leave the agency with you. But, no, that's not what I meant. What I meant was she spotted you when you broke into my Trading House."

"She found her way back to Darlington, did she?" Cimarron shifted his reins from his right to his left hand as, behind him, Tracy's horse snorted again.

"She did. She saw you take the Indian kid with you."

Cimarron remained silent.

"Loretta said you left her in some trees last night and went gunning for some horse thieves. She said she saw you shoot one of them. That alarmed the lady so she ran right back to where she belonged—to me."

Cimarron watched Drake's hand come to rest on the butt of his revolver. The man's itching for a scrap, he thought. Well, I'm ready to give it to him.

"She was real repentant, Loretta was," Drake commented. "She told me she'd been wrong about you—that you were a killer and she wanted nothing more to do with you. She said how sorry she was that she went and told you—told you things about me and Enoch she oughtn't've told you or anybody else for that matter."

"You're talking about the two sets of books you keep, is that it, Drake? About how you and your partner Tracy here cheat both the Indians and the government while fattening up your own purses."

"Loretta's a flighty woman," Drake remarked offhandedly. "Too trusting by far. I told her she should never have taken up with a man who's a born troublemaker if I ever saw one."

"You came out here to fight me over Loretta?"

"We came out here to kill you," Tracy said, and as Cimarron glanced over his shoulder at the agent, he saw the revolver in Tracy's hand. "Drop your gun," Tracy ordered. "Your rifle."

Cimarron looked back at Drake and saw the gun in the man's hand that was aimed at him, and the triumphant smile on Drake's face.

"It wouldn't do," Drake said, still smiling, "for you to go and tell anybody else what Loretta told you about the pair of us. Why, it could ruin our reputations if word of our private enterprise got spread about."

"So you two decided you'd best kill me and have done with it, is that it?"

"That's it," Drake said almost amiably.

"Your revolver and rifle," Tracy barked at Cimarron. "Drop them."

Cimarron pulled his Winchester from his boot. "Don't shoot me, Tracy. You can see I'm handing over my rifle. Drake, take it."

He thrust the rifle toward Drake and when Drake reached out to seize it, Cimarron rammed its barrel against the head of Drake's mount, causing the horse to swing to one side and step back quickly.

Cimarron leaped from the saddle and shoved his horse around so that it was between him and Tracy. He reached out, seized Drake's left boot, and yanked on it, pulling Drake out of his saddle.

Cimarron crouched behind the black, pulled Drake up, twisted the man's right arm behind his back and then, with Drake in front of him as a shield, he stepped out from behind the black.

"You shoot, Tracy, and it's your partner you'll kill," he said in a harsh voice as he unholstered his Colt.

Tracy didn't hesitate. He fired.

His bullet slammed into Drake's body, and as it did Cimarron thrust Drake toward Tracy, dropping down on one knee.

His finger squeezed the trigger of his .44 but, as he fired, Drake staggered backward and fell against him, sending his shot clear of Tracy.

Cimarron swiftly hauled the dying Drake to his feet and, once again using the man's limp body as a shield, fired at Tracy at the same instant that the agent fired at him.

Tracy succeeded only in killing Drake.

When Cimarron fired at him a third time, grazing his shoulder this time, Tracy wheeled his horse and galloped away, heading north.

Cimarron dropped the dead Drake and, cursing himself for having believed that there was any honor among thieves, leaped into the saddle of the black and, his revolver still in hand, set out in pursuit of Tracy.

The agent, riding hard, soon lengthened the distance between himself and Cimarron, who cursed the black he was riding, Tracy, and himself for having let Tracy escape.

He spurred the black, willing it to run—to fly—and the pony did its best, but its best, Cimarron realized, was just not good enough to compete with Tracy's long-legged and evidently strong-winded horse.

I'm losing the bastard, Cimarron thought. He's getting away from me, dammit!

As he rode on after Tracy, Cimarron saw him top a low rise and then start down it, but before he was lost to sight, Tracy turned his horse, rode to the crest of the rise and then down it and on toward Cimarron, who exclaimed aloud, "Now, what the hell . . ."

He slowed the black slightly as Tracy continued toward him and then, as if the agent had realized that he was making a mistake, he veered sharply to the left.

Cimarron, as he tugged on the black's reins and rode to the right after Tracy, heard the sound of shooting. A moment later, he stared in disbelief as a small band of Cheyenne warriors topped the rise on his left and rode down it.

War Pony, he thought, recognizing the leader of the band. Where the hell does he think he's going?

When he was almost upon Tracy, he fired a warning shot and yelled, "Hold it, Tracy, or the next one'll bust your skull wide open!"

Tracy slowed his horse and then halted, his shoulders drooping, his head hanging down. He was breathing heavily as Cimarron rode up to him and said, "Throw down that gun, Tracy. You won't be needing it anymore." When Tracy had done so, Cimarron looked back to find War Pony and the men with him dismounting and setting up a ragged skirmish line as riders—Cimarron guessed there were at least a dozen of them—topped the rise.

"We're joining up with those Cheyennes," he told Tracy. "Move out."

As both men rode toward the Indians, the riders coming down the rise opened fire and the Cheyennes returned it, forcing their attackers to turn and disappear behind the rise.

"What's going on " Cimarron asked War Pony when he reached him.

"Rumson."

"What's he after you for?"

War Pony shrugged and fingered the elk's tooth he wore on a piece of rawhide looped about his neck.

"Where's the rest of your people?"

"We saw Rumson and his men coming," War Pony replied. "Women and children and some men run to mountains. Hide there. We come south."

"Tracy," Cimarron said to the agent, "you'd best get your ass out of that saddle or it'll be shot out of it if those cowboys come back."

Cimarron dismounted at the same time that Tracy did and, crouching behind the hunkered-down agent, said, "I'd as soon shoot you as one of those cowboys, so don't try anything fancy."

"I could go and have a talk with Rumson, War Pony," Cimarron suggested, but War Pony vigorously shook his head. "You're determined to kill them?"

War Pony made no response.

"You're outnumbered. There must be a dozen of them. Maybe more. You're just five."

War Pony maintained his silence as time passed and Cimarron considered his next move. Leave and take Tracy with him? The thought sired another one.

"War Pony, the cavalry's coming. You hang around here much longer, you're going to get yourselves caught in a crossfire."

"Not long now."

"What the hell are you talking about?"

Several minutes passed and then War Pony pointed to the rise.

Cimarron watched Rumson and his men, who were walking down the rise, their hands held high above their heads and their holsters empty. He was about to question War Pony when a band of mounted Cheyennes appeared on the rise carrying guns and herding the horses they had obviously taken from their prisoners as they marched them toward where War Pony and the four other Cheyennes stood waiting beside Cimarron.

"You told me the rest of your men went with the women and children to the mountains," he said to War Pony.

"When women and children safe, the men chase Rumson and his men. It was our plan."

"Clever tactics," Cimarron admitted, and stood up as Rumson strode up to him.

"You!" Rumson snarled, glaring at Cimarron. "I might've known you'd have had a hand in this."

Cimarron ignored the accusation. "Why'd you go after these Cheyennes?"

"To kill us," War Pony snapped angrily.

Rumson answered, "A whole mess of them were on my range ready to raid my herd."

"No cattle raid," War Pony said, standing toe to toe with Rumson. "We go north—home."

"That's the truth," Cimarron said. "They're heading up into Nebraska. Maybe Dakota Territory. They've left the reservation, so you're problem's solved."

"I haven't been paid for those beeves you stole from me," Rumson countered.

"You will be, but that wasn't my point. I'm trying to tell you that there'll be a lot less Indians on the Cheyenne-Arapaho reservation now so they won't be pestering you for beef as often. You ought to be escorting these fellows on their journey instead of trying to drive them back."

"I can't say I'm sorry to see the sonsabitches go," Rumson muttered.

"You're glad to see them go."

"You're damned right I'm glad."

"Then maybe you'd be willing to help them on their way," Cimarron said speculatively, an idea forming in his mind.

"What've you got in that tricky mind of yours?"

Instead of answering Rumson's question, Cimarron turned to War Pony. "Your women and children, they're in the Glass Mountains?"

War Pony nodded.

"Tell you what you do. You and your men ride northeast until you hit the Cimarron River—"

War Pony interrupted, "Mountains in north."

"Hold on a minute. Now, just hear me out on this. You ride northeast till you come to the river. You ride into it and then northwest to hide your trail. Once you're past the mountains you leave the river and come down south into the mountains, collect your women and children, and ride north again. That way, with Rumson's help, the cavalry'll have little chance of finding your trail."

"My help?" Rumson bellowed incredulously.

"These Cheyennes can give you and your men back your guns and horses. Then, once they leave, you set your men—

some of them—to riding behind them for a spell to wipe out their trail. Then we'll all sit tight right here till the cavalry shows up and we'll tell them that we spotted the Cheyennes heading due West.''

''You're asking my help and all I want to do is get even with you for hanging me and my two boys up by the heels and rustling my beeves.''

''See that fellow hunkered down there?'' Cimarron pointed to Tracy.

Rumson's eyes widened as he noticed Tracy for the first time. ''When am I going to get paid?'' he roared at the agent.

''I'll see to it that he pays you,'' Cimarron declared. ''Soon,'' he added.

''All right,'' Rumson agreed. ''When are these bucks moving out?''

''Now,'' Cimarron said. ''That sound all right to you, War Pony?''

''We go,'' War Pony answered, and moments later the Cheyennes were riding up the rise.

Rumson ordered several of his men to ride behind the Indians to obliterate the trail left by their unshod ponies.

At sundown, the cavalry appeared in the south and Rumson said, ''It's about time. Some Indian chasers they are. Those redskins could be close to the Kansas border by now.''

Kendrick, as he rode up, halted his men. ''Cimarron, what are you doing here?'' he asked, obviously bewildered.

''I've been chasing Tracy,'' Cimarron answered. ''I mean him and Drake were chasing me first but—it's a long story, Kendrick. You're looking for the Cheyennes and Mr. Rumson and me, we can tell you where they went.''

''That's right, Lieutenant,'' Rumson said with a crafty glance at Cimarron. ''They got their squaws and kids holed up somewhere in the Glass Mountains. A bunch of bucks tried to rustle some of my beef and we ran them off earlier today. They're heading for the mountains too.''

''God *damn* you, Rumson!'' Cimarron shouted, and was about to make a grab for the man but suddenly thought better of it. Turning quickly, he said, ''I'm turning Tracy over to you, Kendrick.'' Before Kendrick could respond, Cimarron was in the saddle and riding up the rise.

11

Got to find those Cheyennes, Cimarron thought as he rode into the Glass Mountains. Got to move them out so they can link up with War Pony and his men who'll be coming down from the north by and by.

Dusk was deepening into darkness as he began searching for the camp of the Cheyennes. It'll be hidden real good, he told himself, and rode into a space that was more of a deep cleft in the side of one of the mountains than a canyon. Finding it empty, he rode out again as the first stars appeared in the sky. As he continued searching, the crescent moon began to rise.

He came to a thick stand of timber that covered the slope of one of the mountains and he dismounted, intending to lead his black through the trees. Are they hiding in there, he asked himself. He considered calling out in the hope of getting a response from the Cheyennes but rejected the idea. Wouldn't work, he thought. I let out a yell, it'll more'n likely send them deeper into cover than it'll help to flush them out.

A weak and distant wail reached him and he smiled as it ended in a wet gurgle. Baby, he thought. Somewhere up ahead in these trees. Somebody just squelched it. He moved on in the direction from which the sound had come.

He had taken only a few steps when he heard a faint whisper of sound behind him. But, before he could turn, someone leaped out of the underbrush at him and he caught the flash of moonlight on a knife blade. He dodged the blade as it slashed at him and seized the knife-wielder by the wrists, shaking and squeezing the right one.

"Antelope!" he exclaimed in surprise as the knife fell from her hand. "It's me!"

"Cimarron?"

"Glad I got you before you gutted me. Where's your camp?"

"Up the slope."

"You were standing guard?"

Antelope nodded and picked up her knife.

"Come on. Let's go to your camp. You people've got to get out of here. The cavalry's coming."

"War Pony? The men with him?"

"I ran into them back on the trail. They're on their way here." Cimarron ducked under a low-hanging branch, still leading the black, Antelope several paces ahead of him.

"Why do you come?" she asked him.

"Came to warn you. You all'll have to head north. Tonight. I don't think the cavalry'll risk coming into these mountains at night. They'll more likely wait till dawn to come after you."

Cimarron stepped to one side to avoid a deadfall and, as he did so, a shot rang out, barely missing him.

"What the hell!" he exclaimed, drawing his Colt.

An unseen woman shouted something in the Cheyenne language and Antelope quickly shouted back.

"I'm a friend of yours!" Cimarron said to Antelope, exasperated. "I wish to hell you ladies would stop trying to kill me!"

Warrior Woman emerged from behind a loblolly pine and strode toward Cimarron and Antelope, a rifle cradled in her arm.

"I told her not to shoot," Antelope whispered to Cimarron as he holstered his Colt. "She told me to run when she fired at you. She thought I was your prisoner."

"Howdy," Cimarron said to Warrior Woman when she came up to him, her expression grim.

She grunted and then spoke in Cheyenne to Antelope.

"She wants to know what you do here," Antelope told Cimarron.

"Tell her War Pony and his men are coming down into the mountains from the north. Tell her everybody's got to move out to meet them. Right away."

Antelope translated Cimarron's message and he was annoyed to find that Warrior Woman was shaking her head.

She spoke and then Antelope translated her words. "Warrior

158

Woman says War Pony gave orders not to leave mountains because Big Eagle is dying.''

"Dammit, you're *all* liable to die if you don't get out of here before those troopers get here. Tell the lady that.''

Antelope did, but Warrior Woman merely shook her head again.

Cimarron swore.

Warrior Woman spoke to Antelope, who then told Cimarron, "She says we must go back to guarding the camp.''

"Tell her I got a better idea.'' He quickly explained it to Antelope who then spoke to Warrior Woman, who briefly considered what she had heard and then stalked away.

"She knows the spot I told you about?''

When Antelope shrugged, Cimarron hurried after Warrior Woman but he didn't catch up with her until she was standing above the cleft he had searched earlier.

"Antelope, you tell her this is what we're going to do.''

When Antelope had translated Cimarron's words, Warrior Woman put down her rifle and began to roll a heavy boulder toward the spot that he had indicated.

As he, with Antelope's help, dislodged another boulder and began to roll it up into position beside Warrior Woman's, he said, "We've got to get the biggest ones we can find. The three of us ought to be able to pile up a whole bunch before we're through.''

When the crescent moon was directly overhead, they had done so and Cimarron nodded in satisfaction. "Now then. This next part's the real tricky one.'' He told Antelope what they must do and Antelope spoke to Warrior Woman, who almost smiled at Cimarron as she listened.

"Now that you two've got your part in this straight, I'll be moving out.''

"When will you come back?'' Antelope asked anxiously.

"Soon's I find the cavalry's camp and finish what I'm setting out to do.'' He stepped into the saddle and started down the slope of the mountain.

Minutes later, he was riding through the long grass that covered the plain and peering into the distance as he searched for the cavalry's camp.

The stars above him in the dark arc of the sky seemed close enough to touch and the crescent moon was a silver sliver, the moon's remainder a ghostly grayness. The grass swished faintly against his boots and the black's legs as he rode on. A light breeze was blowing, almost cooling the night, and it carried to Cimarron the sound of a fox barking far away.

Did the cavalry turn back? He considered the question. No, he decided. They must be camped somewhere and that somewhere had to be in the direction he was riding—south. But where were the troopers?

When he spotted a dull red glow just this side of the horizon, he knew he had his answer. They were there where that fire burned low. He halted the black and sat his saddle, closing his eyes for a moment to sharpen his night vision and then opening them again.

The campfire shed little light. It was, in fact, almost out. The light it gave came mostly from embers rather than flames, but that light was enough to enable Cimarron to make out the men sleeping on the ground near it. He moved closer to the camp, walking the black, as he searched for the horses. He finally spotted them on the right side of the camp, each of them tied to a long rope that ran between two distant trees. He rode to the right and, once he was well beyond the horses, he dismounted and, leaving the black with its reins trailing, got down on all fours and began to crawl through the grass toward the horses—and the trooper who had been assigned to guard them.

The breeze shifted direction and began to blow the grass into Cimarron's face as he crawled on, feeling the ground ahead of him in order to avoid any twigs that might snap under him and betray his presence. He halted as the breeze brought the pungent odor of manure to his nostrils. He raised his head slightly until he could see above the grass and, when he had located the guard's position, he crawled on toward the man. When he heard footsteps, he stopped again and drew his Colt. Gripping it by the barrel, he waited and, when the guard was about to pass the spot where he crouched, he suddenly leaped to his feet and struck the man's skull with the butt of his gun.

The guard groaned and his knees buckled.

Cimarron seized him and lowered him to the ground. Kneeling beside him, he used his bandanna to gag the man and then, pulling two piggin strings from the pocket of his jeans, he bound the man's ankles and wrists with them.

Then he rose and moved stealthily toward the nearest tree

160

to which the rope holding the troopers' mounts was tied. He pulled his knife from his boot—and froze as one of the sleeping men in the distance sat up, threw off his blanket, and got to his feet.

He remained motionless as the man walked some distance from the camp and urinated. Only when the man was back in his place with his blanket wrapped around him again did he sever the rope. Swiftly, he moved down the long line of horses, whispering meaningless words to them to keep them as quiet as possible, until he reached the other tree to which the rope was tied. He severed the rope and then, gripping the end of it in his right hand, he moved out, still whispering to the horses and stroking the nose of the nearest one. He moved slowly, step by sure step, and the horses, tied to the long rope by looped ropes around their necks, followed him.

One in the middle of the line suddenly nickered.

Cimarron tensed but kept moving because he knew he mustn't stop now. "Good boys," he whispered to the horses. "We're going to make it. You just wait and see if we don't."

And then, upon reaching his black, he climbed into the saddle, still gripping the rope. He wheeled the animal and walked it west until he was certain he had gone far enough so as not to be heard by any of the troopers in the camp. Only then did he turn the black and ride north toward the mountains, the horses strung out in a long line behind him.

He spurred the black and galloped on through the foothills until he reached the cleft that had been his destination. He let go of the rope and the horses went galloping on into the cleft. He rode back and came up behind the last of them in order to herd them into the deep cleft that was a reasonable facsimile of a box canyon.

He halted at its entrance, looked up, and saw the two figures silhouetted against the starry sky and he called out, "*Now!*"

Turning his horse, he rode up the slope. Behind him he heard the sound of the first boulder crashing down. When he reached the top of the slope, he leaped out of the saddle, put his shoulder against one of the boulders, and heaved. It went over the side and hit the ground below.

He, Warrior Woman, and Antelope continued to send boulders over the edge of the cleft and when they were all gone Warrior Woman let out a cry of triumph.

161

Cimarron got back into the saddle and rode down the slope. When he reached the bottom, he surveyed the entrance to the cleft and then, when he was satisfied that the rocky blockade was sufficiently high to keep the horses from escaping, he returned to Warrior Woman and Antelope.

"You two'd best keep on standing guard here," he told Antelope. "I don't think those soldier boys'll be giving you any trouble tonight but it's best to be safe instead of sorry. Will you point me the way to your camp?"

Antelope did and, after touching the brim of his hat to the two women, he rode toward it over slopes and down into gullies and then back up the side of the mountain again.

Long before he reached the camp, he heard the shrill cries and occasional shrieks that were coming from it. Those women keep that up, he thought, and General Sheridan himself'll hear it and come after them.

Moments later, as he rode into the camp that was situated in the middle of a clearing on the north side of one of the mountains, he saw the reason for the noise, which, he realized, was being made by the women as they mourned.

Many of them were slashing their foreheads and legs with sharp knives. Blood poured from their wounds. Some of the grief-stricken women were hacking off their hair.

Cimarron sat his saddle, staring down at Big Eagle who, dressed in a fine pair of buckskin leggings, lay on his back on the ground. On his feet were beaded moccasins. His hair had been neatly braided and adorned with a white eagle feather. His hands were folded across his chest and on his closed eyes rested two small pebbles.

War Pony stood staring down at his dead father. Behind him, Nine Fingers and several other Elk Soldiers stood motionless and expressionless.

The wailing rose and fell as the woman mourned. Their knives glinted in the moonlight as they continued to mutilate themselves.

Cimarron got out of the saddle and walked up to where War Pony stood. "I'm real sorry," he said softly.

"Big Eagle walks the Hanging Road tonight," War Pony said, and looked up at the Milky Way.

"Your women," Cimarron said, "they're acting like Big Eagle was killed in battle the way they're cutting themselves up so fierce."

"Big Eagle did die in battle," War Pony declared emphatically. "The women know it. I know it. He died in the battle we all fought on the reservation. No blood. No bullets. But a battle."

Cimarron understood and, understanding, thought of the scrawny cattle that had been provided to the Cheyennes, of the annuities Tracy and Drake had stolen, of the idleness of men who had once been warriors and who now could do little more than sit as their days passed and their world died around them before first sickness and then death came to them in their despair and were welcomed as friends.

He thought of buffalo hunters who killed not only buffalo but the animal that had once supported an entire civilization. He thought of whiskey and of demoralized men like Walks with Wolves who would trade their daughters for it.

"War Pony—" he began, but War Pony turned away from him and spoke in Cheyenne to the Elk Soldiers behind him.

Cimarron watched as the men began to build a scaffold in a nearby tree's branches. He watched as War Pony wrapped his father in a blanket and carried the old man to the scaffold and placed him in it. He watched Nine Fingers bring up a roan which War Pony killed with a single rifle bullet and left lying beneath the scaffold.

Big Eagle's horse, he thought and then went up to War Pony. "I don't mean no disrespect," he said, but you people have got to get moving." He quickly told War Pony what had happened and concluded, "Those troopers won't have a whole lot of trouble finding their horses and once they do and get them out of their trap they'll be after you again."

"We go," War Pony said.

"Hold on a minute. Your people are going to need a good head start and I think I know how you can have yourselves one."

"Speak."

Cimarron did, and when he had finished, War Pony said, "Elk Soldiers go with you. Crazy Dogs, Bow Strings—others go with women and children." He beckoned to Nine Fingers and, when the man had joined him, he spoke to him in Cheyenne.

Moments later, as Nine Fingers shouted orders in the Cheyenne language, the wailing of the women subsided and the people made ready to move out. The men mounted their horses and the women, carrying babies and bundles, began to leave the camp, guarded by the men of the soldier societies who rode ahead of and behind them and along each flank of the line that was quickly lengthening as more and more women moved out.

Cimarron, when the camp was almost deserted, rode out into the night with War Pony and a small band of Elk Soldiers. When they reached the slope above the cleft in which the horses were still trapped, they halted and dismounted.

As Warrior Woman and Antelope materialized out of the darkness, War Pony ordered them back to the camp. Warrior Woman promptly obeyed his order, disappearing into the darkness from which she had just emerged, but Antelope walked up to Cimarron and, when he noticed her, she asked, "You come north with us?"

"Nope. When I'm through here I'm heading back to Arkansas."

"I make you good woman."

Cimarron, aware that War Pony was covertly watching him, said, "I've no doubt in the world that you'd do that, honey. But it's not to be."

"I go to Arkansas with you."

Cimarron shook his head. He put his hands on Antelope's shoulders. "I like you and you like me. We met but now we have to part. War Pony'll look out for you."

As Antelope glanced in the Cheyenne's direction, War Pony busied himself giving orders to the Elk Soldiers who were taking cover behind trees and beneath rocky outcroppings.

"He's a good man, Antelope."

"My father—I told him I—but he gave me to Warrior Woman. She had more horses to give for me than War Pony did."

"Your father's back on the reservation with the Southern Cheyennes. And you're a grown-up woman now. Seems to me you're able to make your own choices about important things in your life."

Antelope looked up at Cimarron. "I will remember you. Before you came, I wanted—" She again glanced in War Pony's direction.

"I'll be going before long."

Antelope nodded and then walked over to War Pony. She said something to him, and then vanished in the darkness.

Cimarron went over to where War Pony was standing and said, "Dawn's not far away. The cavalry'll be along soon's we see first light, or I miss my guess."

An hour passed. The stars paled and then faded before vanishing entirely. The crescent moon, looking abandoned, remained visible in the sky until the first pink fingers of the still invisible sun's light touched the cluster of clouds that was hanging just above the eastern horizon, turning them a delicate rose.

"They come," War Pony said, and pointed.

Cimarron, hunkered down behing a pile of stones that had once been a boulder before countless frosts destroyed it, nodded. "You told your men not to shoot to kill?"

"I told them."

"What we've got to do is first run them off and then keep them pinned down. Till noon at least. Longer'd be better. Say midafternoon. That way your people will have had a good chance to cross the Kansas border."

War Pony raised his arm as Cimarron watched the troopers heading for the rocky barrier in the mouth of the cleft behind which were their horses.

"There's nothing a mounted soldier likes less," he commented to War Pony with a grin, "than putting one foot in front of the other on solid ground. Makes him feel like an infantry man and that's not a good feeling for a cavalry man to have."

Minutes later, War Pony dropped his arm and as he did so the Elk Soldiers who were scattered across the slope began to fire their rifles.

The troopers, taken by surprise, ran for cover, but there was little available to them. Most of them scurried around the side of the slope until they were out of sight.

As the firing of the Elk Soldiers continued, Cimarron said, "We've got the advantage over them up here. But they're just liable to send a detail up the mountain to higher ground to try to pick us off."

"Nine Fingers on top of mountain. With two men."

"Good."

The troopers began to return the fire of the Cheyennes, but their ragged barrage was ineffectual principally because they could not see their targets and also because the angle from which they were forced to fire did not give them much of a chance to hit the Indians who were firing on them.

The exchange of fire continued with occasional pauses. Time passed and the sun rose and began to ascend the sky.

A trooper made a dash out into the open, dropped to one knee and fired. The Cheyennes put bullets into the dirt around him and he quickly dived for cover.

Just after noon, Cimarron heard the sound of firing from behind and above him. "Nine Fingers," he said and War Pony nodded. "Kendrick must be fit to be tied by now. No horses. Him and his men pinned down like hides pegged out to dry. Their counterattack beaten back—I hope."

His hope was realized a few hours later when Nine Fingers and the two men who had been with him appeared and took up positions near War Pony.

The Indians spoke together for several minutes and then War Pony told Cimarron, "We go now."

Cimarron nodded. He rose when War Pony did and then they made their way back around the slope to where the ponies had been left.

"I want to wish you a whole world full of good luck." Cimarron held out his hand.

War Pony shook it vigorously.

Nine Fingers reached out and shook Cimarron's hand even more vigorously after which he made the sign for white man and then the sign for friend.

He stepped back then as, one by one, the other Elk Soldiers came up and shook Cimarron's hand.

"Well, I'd best be going now," Cimarron told War Pony.

"Wait. I told you. Elk Soldiers strong men. Brave men."

"You did."

War Pony removed the rawhide thong from around his neck on which the elk's tooth hung, gleaming white in the sunlight. He placed the thong around Cimarron's neck.

"Now you are Elk Soldier. One of us."

Cimarron looked down at the glistening tooth and then up at War Pony. "War Pony does me great honor. War Pony makes me proud."

"We will ask Heammawihio to help you. We will ask Aktunowihio to let you live long and be well. Elk Soldiers will remember how you helped us. It is a good thing to remember a friend."

War Pony turned and mounted his pony. When the other men were also mounted, he gave Cimarron a final glance and then rode down the slope.

When the Cheyennes had disappeared, Cimarron stepped into the saddle of the black and rode down the north side of the mountain. He then rode east for a considerable distance before turning his horse south and then heading north so that he could come up on the trooper's position from behind.

Some time later, as he rode into the foothills of the Glass Mountains and hailed Kendrick, Kendrick turned and stared at him in surprise.

Cimarron rode up and dismounted. "We do seem to keep running into each other, don't we, Lieutenant?" He watched the troopers—and Tracy—struggling to remove the boulders from the entrance leading to the cleft in the mountain. "You had some trouble here, did you?"

"Our horses were stolen last night," Kendrick replied. "We awakened to find them gone and the trooper who had been guarding them bound and gagged."

"The Cheyennes did that?"

"Our horses are trapped behind these boulders. Obviously, if it was the Cheyennes who stole the horses, they didn't want them for their own use. Their apparent purpose in stealing them was to slow down our pursuit and, I must say quite candidly, they have succeeded admirably in achieving their objective.

"When we reached this spot at dawn this morning, we were fired upon by the Indians. They kept us pinned down here for hours. But, some time ago, they stopped firing. I sent a man up there to scout the area and he reported no sign of any Indians. Oh, he did find where they had camped—cold fires, ponies' thoroughly dried droppings, that sort of thing."

"Which means the Cheyennes lit a shuck some time back."

"Yes. Those Indians who were firing at us were merely a rear guard who practiced a delaying tactic until the main body of those who had fled the reservation could get a sufficient distance ahead of us."

"Maybe you could catch up with them if you boys ride real hard."

"The sun will be setting before long," Kendrick remarked dolefully, glancing up at the sky. "You know, it's a rather odd thing," he mused as the troopers sent a boulder rolling down from the huge pile. "As we followed the trail of our horses, we found not a single track made by any unshod horses and one would have expected to find the tracks of at least one and probably more unshod horses—Cheyenne ponies, I mean."

Cimarron bent down, plucked a piece of grass, and placed it between his teeth.

"Decidedly odd, wouldn't you say, Cimarron?"

"Odd things happen out here in Indian Territory," Cimarron replied with a shrug of his shoulders.

"It's interesting that you should put it that way because, during the entire skirmish between my men and the Cheyennes, not a single trooper was killed—or even wounded. It was almost as if those Indians were trying not to kill or wound us."

A boulder crashed down to the ground as the sweating troopers and a haggard-looking Tracy continued their work.

"Where did you take off for so suddenly, Cimarron? I mean when Rumson put us onto the Cheyennes?"

"Oh, I had business to tend to."

"And did you tend to it?"

Cimarron thought he caught a glint in Kendrick's eye. The man seemed about to smile. "I tended to it." Did Kendrick suspect, he wondered. It was time to end the palaver while he was still on steady ground. "Well, I figure you'll be camping here tonight, Lieutenant, so I guess I'll head on back to Fort Reno, pick up my prisoner, and ride for Fort Smith."

Kendrick thoughtfully stroked his chin. "Those Cheyennes are probably at or across the Kansas border by now. It seems to me that the judicious thing for me to do at this juncture is to return to Fort Reno and notify General Sheridan about the failure of my mission. Wait a bit, Cimarron, and we'll all ride back together."

It was nearly midnight when they reached the Darlington Agency and, as they forded the Arkansas River, Cimarron noticed a light in Drake's Trading Post. He turned to Tracy and gave the man an order.

With obvious reluctance, Tracy shouted, "*Loretta!*"

A moment later the door of the Trading House flew open and Loretta appeared in the doorway, lamplight streaming out into the night from behind her. "Bob? Is that you?"

"It's Enoch," Tracy replied.

"Howdy, Loretta." Cimarron spoke quickly to Kendrick.

"Miss Croft," Kendrick said, "I have just been informed by this deputy marshal beside me that you have participated with Tracy and Drake in their schemes to cheat the Indians on this reservation of what is rightfully theirs.

"I am told that you are aware of the existence of two separate sets of books kept by Drake. I respectfully submit to you that you may escape arrest if you turn those books over to me now."

Loretta opened her mouth to speak and then closed it. She turned and, her dress whipping about her legs, ran into the Trading House. When she returned several minutes later, she thrust two large ledgers into Kendrick's hands.

"Thank you, Miss Croft. I shall expect you to leave the agency and the reservation itself by noon tomorrow. Should you fail to do so—should you unwisely choose to remain here—I must warn you that you will be subject to arrest on criminal charges of fraud."

"But I can't leave!" Loretta protested. "I'm waiting for Bob to come back from—"

"Trying to kill me," Cimarron interjected. "Well, he did try but I tried harder."

"He shot Bob," Tracy told Loretta. "He killed him."

She gave an anguished cry, her hands flying up to cover her face, as she began to cry. And then, her eyes flashing, she shouted, "It's all your fault, Cimarron! I never should have told you what I did!"

"That's right, honey," he agreed pleasantly. "You never should have and that's a sad fact. What's more, you never should have gone back to Drake. If you hadn't, he wouldn't be dead now, like as not."

With a wail, Loretta disappeared inside the Trading House, slamming the door behind her.

"There's one other matter still to be settled," Cimarron said. "The matter of the hundred head of cattle I took from Rumson's ranch and brought down here to the agency. The man's got to be paid for them."

"That may take some time," Kendrick responded. "God alone knows how long the Bureau will take to appoint a new agent to serve here at Darlington."

"The longer it takes the better as far as I'm concerned,"

Cimarron said. "Let that bastard Rumson sweat some for his money."

"Forward, *ho!*" Kendrick called out and the troopers moved out.

It was still dark when they reached Fort Reno and Kendrick suggested to Cimarron that he spend the remainder of the night at the fort and resume his journey in the morning.

"Much obliged, Kendrick, but I'll ride out tonight. I've got a long trail to travel ahead of me and the sooner I set out on it the better off I'll be."

He shook hands with Kendrick and was about to head for the guardhouse when he turned to Kendrick and asked, "There's something I've been meaning to ask you, Lieutenant."

"Yes?"

"That guard—the one who was looking after your horses. I hope he wasn't hurt too bad."

"He'll be all right, if a bit dizzy for a day or so from the blow on the head you gave him."

"The blow on the head *I* gave him? Kendrick, I didn't—"

Kendrick held up a hand. "I never said anything to you about one of my troopers—the guard—being struck on the head."

Cimarron muttered an oath. "I went and gave the whole damned thing away and all because my memory seems not to be what it should be."

"Did you do it alone or did the Cheyennes help you?"

"I stole the horses. But two ladies of my acquaintance helped block them up in that cleft though."

"I knew almost from the start—from the moment we found the guard—that it must have been you who stole our horses— either by yourself or with some help from your Cheyenne friends."

"How'd you know?"

"I am, I like to think, an observant man, Cimarron," Kendrick said mildly. "I recognized your bandanna that you used to gag the guard. I was certain that no Indian would use piggin strings to tie the man up.

"Then, too, if Indians had stolen our horses we would have seen signs of unshod ponies as I suggested to you earlier.

"Your rather ridiculous explanation of having business to tend to in a place that was inhabited solely by a fleeing band of Cheyennes—well, you can see my point I'm sure, Cimarron. Your prisoner was in the fort's guardhouse. If you had business anywhere it was right here."

"They needed help, Kendrick. They needed somebody to lend them a hand."

"I know they did. I also know that I should place you under arrest for—oh, any number of charges I could name."

"You're going to?" Cimarron asked, making himself ready for a fight or flight.

"I'm not."

"You're not?"

"I'm sure a Cheyenne Elk Soldier could not be kept in our guardhouse. He'd find a way to escape."

"You know—"

"I know you're a member of the warrior society of Elk Soldiers now."

"How?"

Kendrick pointed to the elk's tooth that hung from the rawhide thong around Cimarron's neck.

Cimarron looked down at it. "I clean forgot all about the fact that I was wearing this."

"I recognized it immediately," Kendrick said. "It's a symbol of rank that any brave and decent man would be proud to wear."

"They're not going to make it, Kendrick. Not in the long haul, they're not."

"The Cheyennes? No, I'm very much afraid that they're not. It's a pity, but it's the way it very definitely is and will be. For a time though, they'll prosper in the north."

"For a time," Cimarron repeated and then, "Kendrick, I'm in need of a horse for Farley. I can pay—"

"Tell the trooper guarding the prisoner that you are to be given one and gear for it. My orders."

The two men shook hands a second time and then Cimarron rode to the guardhouse where he waited until Tracy had been placed inside it. Later, when Farley had been provided with a mount and turned over to him, he left Fort Reno, Farley riding ahead of him.

He fingered the smooth elk's tooth, hearing the echo of Kendrick's words concerning it.

It's a symbol of rank that any brave and decent man would be proud to wear.

Cimarron, riding proud, moved on through the night with his prisoner.

SPECIAL PREVIEW

Here is the first chapter from

CIMARRON
AND THE BOUNTY HUNTERS

sixth in the new action-packed
CIMARRON series from Signet

1

The early morning sun glinted on the surface of the Arkansas River and Cimarron, as he walked along Fort Smith's waterfront, closed his eyes momentarily against the glare.

He fervently wished he could clear his head of the giddiness whirling within it as a result of the previous night's debauchery.

He had sat up until nearly dawn on the opposite bank of the river where the deputies—those not married and living in Fort Smith—camped. There was whiskey. There was beer. And there was talk. He'd told his share of big windies and his extravagant and boisterous lies about his amorous adventures and lawman's escapades were as good and often better than those told by the other deputy marshals.

But now he was paying the price for having drunk too much, talked too loud, and generally caroused, he thought, like a hobo in a whorehouse.

As he turned his head—slowly in order not to dislodge it—

he saw her walking down A Street looking, he thought, just as pretty as a picture. He turned—more of a haphazard swerve than a purposeful change of direction—and went after her.

When he caught up to Rose Collins, he took her arm and she gave him a dazzling smile that almost blinded him.

"Cimarron," she said sweetly. "How nice to see you. You're up early."

"Didn't get to bed down hardly at all last night but don't let's us talk about that. A fool ought to forget his folly as fast as possible. Where do you happen to be headed, Rose?"

"Pritchard's."

"For breakfast?"

"Yes, And you?"

"Pritchard's," Cimarron answered, only then making up his mind to accompany Rose, although breakfast was the last thing in the world he wanted at the moment. He suspected that if he threw any down his stomach would throw it all right back up again.

When they reached the restaurant, he held the door for Rose and, after she had glided past him, he went inside and sat down across from her at the table she had chosen.

The waitress appeared almost immediately, a plain girl wearing a clean white apron over her dark dress. "Yes, please?"

No, thank you, Cimarron thought as he took off his hat, placed it on the table, propped his head in his hands, and muttered, "Coffee. Black as the pit and strong as temptation."

"I'll have some eggs—scrambled," Rose declared brightly, and Cimarron groaned. "Fried potatoes." He swallowed hard. "Stewed tomatoes." He almost retched. "Bread and butter and, of course, coffee."

"Yes, Miss Collins."

"Cimarron, is something wrong?" Rose asked when the waitress had gone, leaning solicitously toward him, a concerned expression on her face.

He started to shake his head, decided that he'd better not risk doing so, and replied, "Nothing a good pine coffin and a six-foot hole in the ground wouldn't cure."

"You poor thing," Rose cooed, patting his hand. "Hangover again?"

"The granddaddy of all hangovers."

"Pretty?"

Cimarron looked up. "This hangover I've got's not the least bit pretty."

"I meant the woman you were drinking with last night."

"I wasn't with a woman," Cimarron said sorrowfully. "Wish to hell I had been. Wish I'd been with you or at least a lady half as pretty as you. There was just a bunch of us deputies with not the sense of a Philadelphia lawyer to spread among the lot of us."

"I should chide you, Cimarron."

"You go right ahead and do that, honey. I know I deserve it. A man should know his limit where liquor's concerned."

"I'm not talking about your drinking habits. I'm talking about the fact that you haven't been to see me in ever so long."

"I did start out last week, Rose—I truly did—but then I realized I didn't have the price to pay you and you know Mrs. Windham don't give credit in her parlor house. Another time— but before I could put one foot in front of the other Marshal Upham sent me hightailing it out into Indian Territory to hunt for a jasper who held up the stationmaster in Boggy Depot."

"What about today—tonight?"

"Maybe. I'm on my way to see Marshal Upham. If he'll take pity on me and won't make me work today, I'll come by Mrs. Windham's and you'll be sure to hear me coming."

"I will?"

"I'll have bells on and I'll be hollering your name out loud so you'll have time to get yourself ready for me."

"I'm not sure that I've ever really been ready for you, Cimarron. You're too unpredictable, not to mention passionate."

They were silent as the waitress placed their orders on the table.

As she was about to withdraw, Cimarron caught her wrist and, looking up into her eyes, asked, "Will you marry me?"

"Beg pardon, sir?"

"I've just now made up my mind to tread the straight and narrow path and you look like a lady who could keep me on it." He slapped the waitress' buttocks lightly and she fled, followed by Rose's gay laughter.

"I declare you are a caution, Cimarron. You've terrified the poor girl."

"She terrified me. Didn't you notice the disapproving looks she was giving me? You'd've thought she was the Virgin Mary and I was a horse thief trying to sneak into Heaven."

As Rose began to eat, Cimarron emptied his coffee cup and stood up shakily.

"Tonight?" Rose prodded with a pert smile.

"We'll see, honey. Glad to have run into you, Rose. You've made this man's mournful morning worthwhile and given me the will to live again."

Cimarron placed a coin on the table, clapped his hat on his head, and, once outside the restaurant, walked slowly down the street. When he reached the stone-walled compound that had been his destination, he entered it and minutes later he was inside Fort Smith's courthouse and knocking on the door of Marshal Upham's office.

"Come in!"

Cimarron opened the door to find Upham standing just inside it. As he dropped down into the nearest chair, Upham gave the door a shove and, as it slammed, Cimarron winced.

Upham walked behind his desk and sat down, studying Cimarron.

"Have I got my hat on backwards?" Cimarron asked gruffly. "Or did I forget to button my fly? You're grinning like a jackass eating cactus, Marshal."

"When's the wake?"

"Do I look that bad?"

"Worse." Upham rummaged about among the pile of papers on his desk, finally found what he had been looking for, and thrust a document at Cimarron.

"Shit, Marshal," Cimarron muttered as he studied the paper Upham had given him, "you can't expect me to go out hunting a murderer considering the condition I'm in. If he so much as spits at me, he'll knock me down for sure and be gone."

"Ernie Wilcox," Upham said, ignoring Cimarron's outburst, "is wanted for murder. The grand jury handed up an indictment and that writ you've got in your hand authorizes you to bring him in dead or alive."

"Marshal, sometimes you talk like somebody straight out of the pages of one of those Beadle and Adams' dime novels. '*Dead or alive.*' Why would I want to bring in this—" Cimarron glanced at the warrant in his hand, "Wilcox dead? The only way I can collect the two dollars for him is if I bring him in alive. Which is not a munificent sum in any man's jeans, I can sure tell you—two dollars isn't."

"Judge Parker, as you know, has repeatedly asked the federal government to authorize higher fees for the work you deputies do."

"Two dollars," Cimarron fumed. "A ribbon clerk makes more money in a year than I do. Some drifters do."

"Ernie Wilcox killed a man in a shootout in McAlester. Witnesses testified to that effect before the grand jury—eyewitnesses. It's an open and shut case. He'll undoubtedly be convicted when he's tried and then Maledon will have his chance to hang the man."

"Two dollars's not enough even to pay for the company of Miss Rose Collins."

"Cimarron, you're not listening to me."

"Wilcox. Witnesses—*eye*witnesses. Warrant." Cimarron held it up and waved it. "I heard you, Marshal. Did you hear me?"

"If you mean did I hear you and your complaints, which have become close to habitual, not to mention tedious, lately, yes, I did. Why don't you stop by the Paris Emporium here in town?"

A puzzled frown appeared on Cimarron's face. "What the hell for?"

"They might have need of another ribbon clerk."

"I'm a sick man this morning, Marshal. It don't seem right that you should be taunting me when I'm on the verge of expiring."

"It's a damn shame about Wilcox," Upham mused, leaning back in his chair and folding his hands across his ample stomach.

"What is? That he killed somebody?"

"The somebody he killed, as you'll learn if you'll read that writ you're holding, was named Louis Labrette, a fur trapper in his early days, a gambling man of late. Yes, the murder itself was a shame but that's not what I was referring to. Witnesses estimated Wilcox's age as no more than sixteen or seventeen. It's a shame to see a youngster like that end his life on the gallows before he's even had a chance to properly live it."

"A body—man or boy—who's quicker to draw a gun than he is to think—well, age don't make the difference. Hot blood's what does. Somebody once said—I read it somewhere—that you can take anything you want just so long as you pay the price for it. Well, this Wilcox fellow went and took what he wanted—a man's life—and now he's got to pay the price for it—if I don't die of a bad case of having no common sense before I can lay hands on him. Reminds me of that other murder case you sent me out on last year. The Fairfax case. Cele Fairfax was a woman and you'd've thought butter wouldn't melt in her mouth but she went and killed two of her boarders

177

up near Fort Gibson. A man can never tell about people, including sixteen-year-olds, and I reckon he'd best not try to."

"If you have quite finished your heartwarming homily, Cimarron, may I suggest that you set out at once for McAlester."

"Well, the spirit's sure willing, Marshal."

"But the flesh is weak?"

"More like at death's door is what it is. I swear I'll never touch another drop of the ardent."

Upham threw back his head and erupted in laughter. "That reminds me of the time you swore you would never lay hands on another woman as long as you lived."

"I sincerely meant it at the time."

"Beth Clinton gave you a run for your money."

"You got it all wrong, Marshal. She ran *with* my money."

When Upham's laughter had subsided, he commented, "You're incorrigible, Cimarron."

"I'm warning you, Marshal. I'm fixing to buy me a dictionary one of these days and when I do I'm going to look up every last one of those names you're always slapping on me and if they turn out to mean what I think they mean—well, you'd best watch your step 'cause I'll come after you with a bar of soap to wash out that nasty mouth of yours. Why, the idea! Calling me things like 'obstreperous' and 'intractable.' And what was that last one? Incor—what?"

"Incorrigible. It means that you are incapable of being reformed."

"How the hell do you expect me to ever be reformed," Cimarron inquired innocently and with a faint grin, "when you're all the time sending me out to keep company with murdering men like this here Ernie Wilcox? They're a bad influence on me, Marshal, and I thought an educated man like yourself ought to be able to see that clear as day."

"Cimarron," Upham said soberly, rising from his chair, "you be careful out there now. Wilcox is a desperate and therefore a dangerous man. He has threatened to kill any lawman who comes after him. Several people heard him make that threat and they are convinced that he is perfectly capable of carrying it out. I wouldn't want to lose the best damned deputy this court has ever had working for it."

Cimarron rose and started for the door. Before he went through it, he turned and said, "Don't you go worrying none about me, Marshal. I'm always careful. Got to be. With the small-size brain that the good Lord saw fit to dole out to me—well, being careful's my only ace in the hole. Be seeing you, Marshal."

Cimarron rode into McAlester the following morning after having camped out the night before under a cloudy sky that was occasionally illuminated by flashes of heat lightning.

He headed for the depot and, when he reached it, he got out of the saddle and wrapped the reins of his black around the hitch rail in front of the wooden building that had a sign above its entrance which read: Lunch and Hot Coffee.

Once inside the building, he sat down at a table near the door and, when a man with a handlebar mustache approached him and asked him what he wanted, he answered, "Information, Hastings."

"The sign outside says we serve lunch and coffee."

"Read it. It happens I don't want neither your lunch nor your coffee. Been here before, you may recall, and had both but I recovered. Where can I find—"

Hastings turned and began to walk away from the table.

Cimarron sprang to his feet, kicked a chair out of his way that crashed to the floor, and seized Hastings by the shoulders. He spun him around and sent him hurtling into the wall.

"Hey, damn you—"

"Sit down, Hastings." Cimarron pointed to a chair and Hastings slid into it, his eyes wary. "Now, then. I'll just resume my seat right here beside you and you can tell me where I'm liable to find Ernie Wilcox, who's a citizen of your fair city."

"I don't know where he is. Haven't seen him in days."

"You know I'm a deputy marshal, don't you, Hastings?"

"I know. You were wearing your badge the last time you came barging in here."

"I'm here to bring Wilcox to Fort Smith for trial on a murder charge. Now maybe you'd like to tell me what you know about this fracas between him and Labrette."

"It happened in the alley that runs alongside the livery stable. Wilcox and Labrette met and they got into an argument. There were people on the streets and some of them saw Wilcox shoot and kill Labrette."

"What was the argument about?" Cimarron asked, hoping to learn something—anything—that might give him a lead concerning the present whereabouts of Ernie Wilcox.

"Esther Lane."

"Who's Esther Lane?"

"A girl."

"Figured as much since I never have yet met a man named Esther." Cimarron's face darkened and he reached out and seized a fistful of Hastings' shirt. "I'm going to shake you till your teeth rattle if you don't stop leading me all the way around the barn and do start getting directly to the point. Who's Esther Lane?"

"She was Ernie Wilcox's girl. Labrette had his eye on her though and Wilcox didn't like it. He'd told Labrette to stay away from her. Labrette didn't. They had words. You know the rest."

"I don't know much of anything yet. This Wilcox, he was a gunslick?"

Hastings shook his head. "Just a kid head over heels in love and hot under the collar about what he thought was Labrette's moving in on what he claimed as his territory—on Esther. Why, that boy was hanging around her house every spare minute he had looking like a lovelorn loon. An armed posse couldn't have chased him away from her. The funny part though's that Wilcox didn't know that Esther had taken a shine to Dan Packer and not Labrette."

"Where might I find this Dan Packer?"

"He lives with his mother—she's a widow—on the east side of the tracks."

"Much obliged." Cimarron rose and left the building. He crossed the tracks of the Missouri, Kansas and Texas Railroad, leading his black, and asked the first man he met where the Widow Packer lived. When the house had been pointed out to him, he went up to it and, leaving the black with its reins trailing, knocked on the front door.

The door was opened by a man Cimarron was sure wouldn't see thirty again. "Dan Packer?"

"I'm Packer. Who are you?"

Cimarron pulled his badge from his jeans, displayed it, and then pocketed it again. "I'm hunting Ernie Wilcox. You happen to know where he is?"

"No."

"When's the last time you saw him?"

"Some days ago. He seems to have left town."

"Which leaves you sitting in the catbird seat where Miss Esther Lane's concerned."

"My relationship with Miss Lane is none of your business, Deputy."

"Maybe you're right about that. Where do you suggest I start looking for Wilcox?"

"Couldn't say. But he'd better not come back here to McAlester and start pestering Miss Lane again."

"You'll run him off if he does?"

"I will."

"You do that and, from what I've heard, you're liable to wind up as dead as Labrette did when he started cozying up to Miss Lane."

"I'm not afraid of any fool kid."

"Maybe you should be. Guns in the hands of fool kids can cause one helluva lot of grief, as Labrette found out. Where can I find Esther Lane? I want to have a talk with her."

"She can't tell you anything."

Cimarron sighed. "Packer, will you do me the favor of letting Miss Lane tell me herself that she can't tell me anything?"

When Packer had given him directions, Cimarron led his horse down the street and tethered it to the picket fence that enclosed the small yard in front of the Lane house. He went up on the porch and knocked on the front door.

"Good day," he said to the young woman who opened the door. He touched the brim of his hat to her, thinking that she wasn't much more than a girl. "Would you happen to be Miss Esther Lane?"

"Yes, I am. But I don't believe I know you."

"My name's Cimarron. I'm a deputy marshal out of Fort Smith. I—"

"You're after Ernie."

"I am." Cimarron noticed that Esther's face had paled. "If we could step inside, maybe you'd be able to tell me something about him that will help me run him to ground."

Esther stiffened, her arms rigid at her sides. "I'll tell you nothing." She began to close the door.

Cimarron thrust out a boot and blocked it. "I know how much you hated him so I thought—"

His ploy worked.

Esther's eyes widened. "Hated Ernie? I didn't. I loved him. I still love him! Oh, I'm so ashamed of myself!" Tears glistened in her eyes.

"You're ashamed of yourself on account of you let Labrette come calling on you which led to Wilcox gunning him down?"

"No, that's not it. Mr. Labrette was no problem as far as I was concerned. He did make himself objectionable for a time but I was finally able to discourage him. It was the way I behaved with Dan Packer that has made me so ashamed of myself. When he first came to town, I thought him rather charming and then he asked if he could call on me and I said he could. He'd been to St. Louis. Even to New Orleans once, he told me. I know he's somewhat older than me—I'm seventeen—but it's the way that two people's spirits touch that's important, not their ages, however different they might be."

"How old is Ernie Wilcox?"

"Eighteen."

"Just a boy."

Esther's eyes flashed. "He's a man, a real man. I know that now. I thought Mr. Packer—he seemed so sophisticated and Ernie, well, he's not seen much of the world and—oh, I was a fool!"

"It's a good thing Wilcox didn't know about your interest in Dan Packer or he'd have like as not gone and gunned Packer down too."

"Don't you dare say a terrible thing like that! Ernie didn't kill Mr. Labrette."

"Witnesses say he did."

"I know they said they saw him shoot Mr. Labrette. But—"

"It's hot out here," Cimarron interrupted. "Couldn't we step inside?"

With obvious reluctance, Esther stepped back and Cimarron entered the front parlor of the house. When they were both seated, he said, "A woman in love's likely to believe all sorts of things about her man. She might even believe he didn't kill a man when other people saw him do it."

"Ernie couldn't kill anybody."

"But he did."

"You said you were a deputy marshal, not a judge."

Cimarron cleared his throat in faint embarrassment. "That picture over there on the table. That's Wilcox?"

Esther reached out, picked up the framed photograph in both hands, and stared at it for a long moment before handing it to Cimarron. "That's Ernie. Oh, how I do wish he would come back." She paused and then, as if she were speaking to herself, added, "He will some day. He promised me he would."

"When there's no likelihood of a man like me being on his trail. Is that what you mean, Miss Lane?" Cimarron returned the photograph to her.

"It was a group of men like you—deputies—who made him run off in the first place. They were coming through town with their prison wagon and Ernie thought for sure they were after him so he came here and he told me he had to leave and—"

"Where'd he say he was going?"

"Do you really think I'd tell you even if I knew? You want to see him hang. You've already decided that he's guilty."

"Whoa there, Miss Lane! You were right before when you said I was no judge. I'm just a lawman with a job to do."

"And that job is to place Ernie Wilcox in the hands of the hangman."

"My job is to take him to Fort Smith," Cimarron corrected, "to stand trial."

"How much do they pay you to do your dirty work?"

"Not near enough."

"How much?"

"Two dollars if I bring him in alive. Nothing if I have to kill him."

Esther gasped. Then, recovering, she jumped up and ran from the room.

Pretty little thing, Cimarron thought, and here I've gone and scared the living daylights out of her.

When several minutes had passed and Esther didn't return, he rose and started for the door. He was opening it when she called his name. He turned to find her holding a small purse in her hand. She snapped it open and pulled out a coin which she held out to him.

"Take it," she said sharply. "Take it and leave Ernie be."

Cimarron's shoulders slumped as he stared at the double eagle Esther was holding out to him. "I can't do that, Miss Lane."

"You can."

"I admit I'm tempted to. I could sure use twenty dollars about now but—" He studied her face. "You love Wilcox a whole lot, do you?"

Esther nodded, tears sliding down her cheeks.

"He's just liable to take a notion to shoot at me when I catch up with him. I'll have to shoot back. You could help him by telling me where he's holed up so I could maybe get the drop on him and avoid—"

"I can't!" Esther wailed and then began to sob. "I can't because I don't know where he is. Oh, please, Cimarron. If you do find him, don't kill him. Please don't, I beg of you!"

"I'll try my best not to but I can't promise you anything. Now, I've got one last question to ask you, Miss Lane. How long's Ernie been gone exactly?"

"Four days."

The sound of Esther's sobs followed Cimarron outside where he stepped into the saddle of his black and rode slowly south along the railroad tracks, considering what he had learned. He knew it wasn't much and he also knew it wasn't enough to put him on Wilcox's trail. He was considering his next move when he noticed the wagon parked behind the depot and the crowd of men gathered around it.

He rode up to the wagon and dismounted, shaking his head. He strode over to the elderly man with the jug in his hands and said, "Pops, you old codger, you never do learn, do you?"

"Cimarron! It's good to see you again!"

"Is it, Pops? You know I got to fine you and then run you off just like I did the last time I caught you up in North Fork Town where you were selling whiskey the same as you're doing here in McAlester right now."

"Selling whiskey? Me? Cimarron, I'm not selling whiskey. What in the world makes you think old Pops Clancy is selling whiskey?"

"That." Cimarron pointed to the Creek who had just handed money to Pops after which Pops partially filled a glass from his jug and then handed the glass to the Indian, who promptly emptied it.

"Let me tell you something, Cimarron," Pops said as he reached into the bed of his wagon, took a potato from it, and handed it to the Creek. "You lawmen are always mighty quick to jump to conclusions. You judge a man far too fast."

"Pops, you're telling me you're *not* selling whiskey? You're telling me my eyes have went and gone bad on me?"

Pops accepted money from another Creek and poured whiskey from the jug into the man's glass before answering Cimarron. "You read the riot act to me up in North Fork Town about how selling whiskey in the Territory's illegal. So I paid the fine you levied on me—though five dollars struck me as a pretty steep price to pay for such a petty offense—and I went and turned over a brand new leaf."

"You stopped selling whiskey, did you?" Cimarron asked in disbelief.

"Sure, I did." Pops handed the Creek he had just given the drink to a potato. "I'm selling potatoes now, Cimarron. Four bits apiece. Anybody who buys a potato off me gets a free drink. Nothing illegal about selling potatoes, now, is there, Cimarron? Or giving my customers a free drink?"

Cimarron exploded in laughter and slapped his thigh. "No, Pops, you old reprobate, I got to admit you're right. It's sure enough legal to sell potatoes in Indian Territory."

"Want to buy one?"

"Sure." Cimarron dug down in his jeans and came up with four bits, which he handed to Pops who filled a glass to the brim, handed it to him, and then gave him a potato, which he had taken from the bed of his wagon.

As Cimarron sipped the whiskey, Pops asked, "Are you still wandering about the Territory looking for evildoers and miscreants?"

"I am, Pops. Thought I'd just caught me my first miscreant on this trip when I spotted you but, like you said, I can't fine or arrest you for selling potatoes."

"Who you after this time?" Pops asked as he filled another glass and handed over another potato to one of his customers.

"Man named Ernie Wilcox."

"Never heard of him."

Cimarron emptied his glass and handed it to Pops. He tossed the potato he was holding in his other hand back into the wagon. "It sure does my heart good to see how you've reformed, Pops. Good luck with your next potato crop. Be seeing you."

Leading his black, Cimarron walked on down the street until he noticed the livery stable on his left. He halted and stared up the alley that ran along one side of the building. He could almost see Wilcox and Labrette standing there and facing one another, their guns drawn. A question suddenly occurred to him.

He went into the livery stable and when a man approached him, he said, "I'd like my horse rubbed down real good and fed. Grain. A mix of oats and barley."

"We'll take good care of him for you, mister. Fine animal, looks like. Looks like you've been riding him hard."

"I have been—all the way from Fort Smith. I'm a deputy marshal. Looking for Ernie Wilcox. Heard he shot a man in the alley next door."

"He did. I saw him do it. Too bad too. Ernie was always such a nice boy."

"Would you mind showing me just how it happened?"

The man, after placing the black in a stall, led Cimarron outside and said. "Ernie he was down there near the end of the alley by those rose bushes that have gone wild. Labrette he was up here at this end. Ernie told Labrette to draw. He did and then both of them fired at each other. Labrette was killed."

Cimarron looked up at the building next door and then at the livery stable.

"Labrette was gut-shot," the stableman said. "You'd have thought Ernie would have plugged him in the lungs."

"Why would you have thought that?"

"Why, because Labrette he was such a little fella. Dapper but small of stature."

"Much obliged to you for taking the time to talk to me. I'll be back to pick up my mount and pay you what I owe."

When the stableman had disappeared, Cimarron leaned back against the wall of the livery, folded his arms, and was soon lost in thought.

Hastings' words came back to him. He recalled Hastings having said that Wilcox had been hanging around Esther's house every chance he got and Esther, he remembered, had said that Wilcox had been gone for four days.

Several minutes later, he made up his mind about the course of action he would follow.

That night found him in a field with his back braced against the trunk of a tree, his eyes on Esther Lane's house at the far end of the field. Time passed. The lamps in the Lane house were extinguished. More time passed.

Finally the night ended and Cimarron rose, stretched, and went in search of breakfast.

But the following night he was back in the field watching the Lane house again. Long before midnight the lamps were extinguished and Cimarron continued to watch the house and surrounding area.

He estimated that an hour had passed, judging by the position of the Pole Star, when he heard a faint sound in the distance. He strained his eyes to see who or what had made it. It had been a harsh scraping sound. He knew where it had come from—the vicinity of the Lane house. He rose, flattening himself against a tree in order not to be seen by anyone who might be sharing the seemingly empty night with him and watched the house, his eyes narrowed.

A shadow that was not a shadow moved across the overhang behind the house on its way toward the single open window facing Cimarron. The upper half of the window, a glassy paleness in the light of the half-moon, suddenly disappeared. When it reappeared, Cimarron loped toward the house and, once behind it, he climbed up on the rain barrel and then onto the overhang, moving carefully in order to make no noise.

He drew his .44 and remained motionless on one side of the window, listening.

Whispers.

A woman's voice. A man's.

He crouched down below the window sill and, propping his gun barrel on it, said, "If you've got a gun, Wilcox, drop it. If I have to shoot at you in the dark, Esther's liable to get hit. Esther, you light a lamp and be quick about it."

When the lamp had been lit and the man in the room, who was, Cimarron was pleased to see, indeed Wilcox, had dropped his revolver, he climbed over the sill.

"Esther," he said, "you get over there against that wall so you won't get hurt." Cimarron bent down and picked up Wilcox's .31 caliber Colt and placed it in his waistband.

"How'd you know I was here?" Wilcox asked him.

Cimarron, aware of Esther's eyes on him, answered, "I kind of figured you'd be showing up here sooner or later. Hoped I'd be here when you did and as it turned out I was."

"But how—" Wilcox persisted.

"I'd been told you spent a lot of time here and Miss Lane told me you'd left town four days ago. I figured that was a long time for a man in love to be away from his woman. I figured you just might sneak back and try to see her. You did and I spotted you. Now then, Wilcox. Did you come here on foot or aboard a horse?"

"I rode in," Wilcox replied, fear twisting his features as he stared at the barrel of Cimarron's gun. "You're a lawman?"

"I am."

"Cimarron!" Esther cried. "Don't take him away from me!"

Cimarron ignored her plea. He gestured with his gun toward the window. "Wilcox, you're going out the same way you came in. I'll be right behind you. Bear that in mind. You run and I'll put a bullet in you. Maybe more than one."

"Ernie!" Esther cried. She ran to him and threw her arms around his neck.

Cimarron reached out, seized her arm, and threw her down on the bed. "Move, Wilcox!"

When Wilcox had gone through the window, Cimarron followed him out onto the overhang. He waited until Wilcox had climbed down onto the rain barrel and then he leaped down to the ground. "Where's your mount?"

"I picketed him over there on the far side of the field."

"Let's go get him."

When they reached the horse, Cimarron waited until Wilcox had freed the animal and then marched him, on foot and leading the horse, to the livery stable where a yawning boy turned Cimarron's horse over to him and Cimarron paid his bill.

As both men rode out of McAlester, Wilcox said plaintively, "I didn't shoot Labrette, Deputy."

Cimarron said nothing.

"I just meant to maybe wound him. Scare him some to keep him away from Esther."

"You'll get to tell your story at your trial," Cimarron said bluntly. "There's no point in your telling it to me. My job's just to bring you in. The rest is up to Judge Parker and the jury."

Marshal Upham looked up as Cimarron strode through the open door of his office. "Did you get Wilcox?"

"I got him. I just turned him and his gun and his horse over to Charley Burns, who's got him locked up by now in the jail down in the basement, no doubt. Charley said you had a letter for me."

"Letter for you? Oh, yes, I do. I have it somewhere here. It was hand-delivered the other day—the day after you rode out, as a matter of fact. Now where did I put it? I know I put it somewhere for safekeeping. The question is where."

Cimarron watched Upham search through the papers on his desk, open drawers, and then slam them shut again. Grinning, he commented, "You sure ought to get yourself organized one of these days, Marshal."

"Here it is!" Upham announced gleefully, pulling a letter out from under his desk blotter. He handed it to Cimarron.

Cimarron took it from him and glanced at his name written on it. He tore the envelope open and took out the single sheet of paper that was inside it.

"What is it?" Upham asked. "Another bill you neglected to pay?" ·

"Listen to this, Marshal. *Whooeeee*, just you listen to this, Marshal D. P. Upham!"

Cimarron began to read the letter aloud. "I have heard extraordinary things about you, Cimarron. I have heard that you never fail to get your man and that—"

"You didn't ever catch that owlhoot—what's-his-name— who tried to rob the Katy Railroad."

"Your memory's slipping, Marshal. What's-his-name, it turned out, fell under the tracks and got run over by the locomotive which nobody thought to tell us when they reported the attempted robbery. Now, don't interrupt me again or I'll be leaving and you never will learn what this lady has written to me."

"Lady?"

"She signs herself Harriet Becker. Now, where was I? Here we go. "—you are a fearless deputy marshal. I am offering you five hundred dollars to track down a murderer. The father of the murdered man will also pay you five hundred dollars if you are successful in your mission. If this matter proves to be of interest to you, please come to see me as soon as possible at the address listed below in Honey Springs."

Cimarron whistled through his teeth and thumbed his hat back on his head. "I'm going to be rich as Croesus, Marshal! Now, what do you think of that?"

"I think that letter raises a number of questions. For example, why didn't this Harriet Becker report the murder she mentions to this office? Honey Springs is, after all, in our jurisdiction."

"You're right. This letter does raise some questions and I'm going to find out the answers to them. But first, since it's near to night, I'm going to pay a social call before I set out for Honey Springs in the morning."

"Knowing you, that can only mean one thing. You're planning to visit Mrs. Windham's so-called boardinghouse—one of the girls there."

"You got it, Marshal, and the first time too. Me and Rose Collins are going to have us a lively little jamboree tonight."

"That's what you call it—a jamboree?"

"What would you call it, Marshal?"

Upham blushed.

About the Author

LEO P. KELLEY was born and raised in Pennsylvania's Wyoming Valley and spent a good part of his boyhood exploring the surrounding mountains, hunting and fishing. He served in the Army Security Agency as a cryptographer, and then went "on the road," working as dishwasher, laborer, etc. He later joined the Merchant Marine and sailed on tankers calling at Texas, South American, and Italian ports. In New York City he attended the New School for Social Research, receiving a BA in Literature. He worked in advertising, promotion, and marketing before leaving the business world to write full time.

Mr. Kelley has published a dozen novels and has several others now in the works. He has also published many short stories in leading magazines.

JOIN THE <u>CIMARRON</u> READER'S PANEL

If you're a reader of <u>CIMARRON</u>, New American Library wants to bring you more of the type of books you enjoy. For this reason we're asking you to join the <u>CIMARRON</u> Reader's Panel, so we can learn more about your reading tastes.

Please fill out and mail this questionnaire today. Your comments are appreciated.

1. The title of the last paperback book I bought was:
   TITLE:_____ PUBLISHER:_____

2. How many paperback books have you bought for yourself in the last six months?
   □ 1 to 3   □ 4 to 6   □ 7 to 9   □ 10 to 20   □ 21 or more

3. What other paperback fiction have you read in the past six months?
   Please list titles: _____
   _____
   _____
   _____

4. My favorite is (one of the above or other): _____

5. My favorite author is: _____

6. I watch television, on average (check one):
   □ Over 4 hours a day □ 2 to 4 hours a day
   □ 0 to 2 hours a day
   I usually watch television (check one or more):
   □ 8 a.m. to 5 p.m.   □ 5 p.m. to 11 p.m.   □ 11 p.m. to 2 a.m.

7. I read the following numbers of different magazines regularly (check one):
   □ More than 6   □ 3 to 6 magazines   □ 0 to 2 magazines
   My favorite magazines are: _____

For our records, we need this information from all our Reader's Panel Members.

NAME:_____

ADDRESS:_____

CITY:_____ STATE:_____ ZIP CODE:_____

8. (Check one) □ Male   □ Female

9. Age (Check one): □ 17 and under   □ 18 to 34   □ 35 to 49
   □ 50 to 64   □ 65 and over

10. Education (check one):
    □ Now in high school   □ Graduated high school
    □ Now in college   □ Completed some college
    □ Graduated college

11. What is your occupation? (check one):
    □ Employed full-time □ Employed part-time □ Not employed
    Give your full job title:_____

Thank you. Please mail this today to:
CIMARRON, New American Library
1633 Broadway, New York, New York 10019